I0819792

TWO LIVING AND ONE DEAD

TVÅ LEVANDE OCH EN DÖD was awarded first prize of ten thousand *kroner* as the best Norwegian novel submitted for the Inter-Scandinavian Literary Contest of 1931.

TWO LIVING AND ONE DEAD

BY

SIGURD CHRISTIANSEN

Translated from the Norwegian by

EDWIN BJORKMAN

GREENWOOD PRESS, PUBLISHERS
WESTPORT, CONNECTICUT

Library of Congress Cataloging in Publication Data

Christiansen, Sigurd Wesley, 1891-1947.
Two living and one dead.

Translation of To levende og en død.
Reprint of the 1932 ed. published by Liveright, New York.
I. Title.
PZ3.C4629Tw8 [PT8950.C55] 839.8'2'372 73-22751
ISBN 0-8371-7348-5

Originally published in 1932 by Liveright, Inc., Publishers, New York

Reprinted with the permission of Liveright

Reprinted in 1975 by Greenwood Press,
a division of Williamhouse-Regency Inc.

Library of Congress Catalog Card Number 73-22751

ISBN 0-8371-7348-5

To avoid any misunderstanding, I wish to make this explanation: The fact that the story is laid in circles connected with the post-office has no ulterior significance. It might as well have been laid in any other field. As a matter of convenience merely, I chose it for the sake of not being troubled by considerations of accuracy.

This post-office, of course, is not to be identified with any particular office. And the characters are my own creation, having no living models.

SIGURD CHRISTIANSEN

June 1931

CONTENTS

I

WHAT HAPPENED

1

ONE Friday evening something happened that startled a whole city and bred consternation everywhere. It was something quite unforeseen, something wildly sensational . . . two armed bandits held up and robbed the city's post-office in true American style.

The first reports had two men killed. This was exaggeration, as one of them had only been knocked out by a blow on the head. But the other one was dead.

Three men were on duty in the office at the time: Berger, Kvisthus, and Lydersen. All of them were between thirty-five and forty. Lydersen alone was not married. He was two years younger than Berger, the oldest one.

The incident occurred shortly after the office had been closed for the day. Two other employees had just started for the depot with the outgoing mail.

That was the reason why those three were alone in the office at the time. Lydersen was putting his cash box into the safe. Kvisthus was on the way to it with the box, while in another room Berger was counting the money-order cash. This was the largest of the three and contained about seven thousand kroner. The other two held, respectively, four hundred and two hundred, the stamps included.

Everything happened with brutal suddenness. The only one who might have told how it started was Kvisthus, who was nearest the rear entrance when the bandits entered. But he was dead. Evidently he had tried to resist and was killed on the spot.

The next one to face the two bandits was Lydersen. As he was about to open the safe, he heard the noise in the next room and rushed out to see what it meant. The key to the safe was still in his hand when he encountered the masked face of a bandit and the muzzle of a gun.

For a moment he stood there as if paralyzed. Then his fright changed into an excited, panicky craving to act, to do something, to negate the facts of the case. At first, in a state of wild agitation, he shrunk back a step. Then he stopped still, and without being clearly conscious of what he did or why he did it, he threw himself at the figure in the doorway. Instinctively he pushed the revolver aside with his left hand, while with his right hand he used the key as a weapon. He knew that he hit something that yielded softly without a sound, and he could hear himself crying out.

He didn't cry for help. What he did was to assert in a rage:

"You dare not shoot! You dare not shoot!"

He kicked and fought, aimlessly and recklessly, until a well-directed blow laid him unconscious on the floor.

Berger did not hear the shot that killed Kvisthus. But he heard Lydersen's screams and the thud of his body as it struck the floor.

The screams made him rise terror-stricken. They were fraught with a penetrating, outraged despair that left no room for misunderstanding. This was no joke. But what was it? What did it mean that some one dared not shoot? Berger made a dash for the door in order to find out and to render assistance if it were needed. There were only three steps to that door, but while he took them he had time to realize that only one thing could be happening outside.

He almost stopped and turned back. The thought of the cash flashed through his mind. That was what they were after . . . whoever they were. It was his duty to protect it, and some one was crying that they dared not shoot. No lives were in danger apparently, and he would have time to hide the money before . . .

Then the air was torn by a last inarticulate cry from the lips of Lydersen, and the sound of his body hitting the floor followed it like a muffled echo, like the thud of a dropped carcass.

Feverishly, angrily, Berger flung the door open, fearful of being too late to prevent whatever was happening.

But on the threshold he halted abruptly, with a sense of shock, his hand still on the door knob. Lydersen was stretched in front of the door like one dead. Behind him stood a strongly built man, his frowning face covered with blood and a black rag drooping from his chin. Quick as a flash this man raised his gun, but even more quickly Berger sprang back and slammed the door in his face.

Wild with fear and rage, Berger picked up the money and made for the window. At that moment the door was pushed open, and he heard behind him a cold, hard, commanding voice:

"Stop, or I shoot!"

Berger put the cash on the window sill and placed himself in front of it, facing the bandit. His lean body swayed back and forth. His face was convulsed by chagrin and excitement.

Then another man appeared in front of him, a few steps away . . . a taller, more youthful figure. The face of this man was entirely hidden by a mask, but his voice rang with ruthless, irresistible determination:

"Get away from the money you are hiding."

Berger did not reply. He stared defiantly at the man and did not move.

"Quick . . . do you hear! No nonsense! We are two men and two guns."

Berger stood still as before.

Then the other one cried in a rage:

"Will you . . . or will you not? One second more, and I shoot!"

One more second Berger hesitated. Then he stepped aside, his face white as a dead man's. Without moving a muscle he saw the stranger empty the cash box with a few rapid and nervous movements. He saw the man disappear through the doorway and heard him lock the door on the outside.

Then he opened the window and jumped to the

street in order to get help. At first he failed utterly. Those to whom he spoke took him for a madman.

2

THIS was all that could be learned about the main incidents of the outrage, and it made the city seethe with excitement during the early evening hours. Everything had happened in less time than it takes to read a brief summary of it. Two unknown men had appeared out of nowhere, had made a clean haul, and had vanished again completely. There was only one known clue. Two men on a motor-cycle had been seen leaving the city in a westerly direction, but their trail was lost a couple of miles beyond the city limits.

Berger and the police found Kvisthus lying unconscious near the rear entrance. Lydersen sat on the floor in a dazed state, blood flowing from a nasty scalp wound. Both were taken to the hospital, where it was found that Kvisthus had suffered a fracture of the skull. The likelihood was that he would die during the night without recovering consciousness. Lydersen was treated and sent home.

From the hospital Berger went to the police station to give whatever information he could. Commissioner Lier was on hand in person to receive his statement. Although everything that could throw the least light on the affair was put down minutely, the resulting report was a meager one. The commissioner read it through with evident disapproval. Then he raised his fishlike eyes. He had the fat, ruddy face of one fond of good living, and he held one hand across his stomach.

"Have you absolutely nothing more to add?"

"No."

"And you suffered no injury at all?"

"No."

The commissioner wrinkled his brow with a painful sense of helplessness.

"You saw nothing of what happened in the other rooms. And you received no injury . . . none at all. In other words, you were, so to speak, not in it?"

Berger's face flushed slightly. So far he had felt confused and lost.

"After all, I was facing a gun."

The hard tone of that reply seemed to provoke the commissioner.

"Ye-es," he said. "And then?"

Berger bowed his head and said nothing.

"You made no effort at resistance?"

"No."

"You gave up the money voluntarily?"

A pale smile flitted across Berger's bewildered face.

"Voluntarily?" he repeated. "Did I give it up voluntarily . . . with a gun against my head?"

The commissioner appeared irritated.

"But you were not shot, were you?"

Berger turned a shade paler as he looked down at his feet.

"No," he said, "fortunately I was not shot."

The commissioner studied him carefully. Suddenly he asked:

"Are you a coward?"

Those words startled Berger, but he looked up uncomprehendingly:

"I was thinking of the others," he said.

"Who put up a fight?"

An expression of pain twisted Berger's thin, boyish face.

"It helped neither them nor the money."

"No, it didn't, but all the same they did what they did."

"Yes, they did. But . . . you ask Kvisthus if he would do the same thing again . . . supposing he had a chance."

The commissioner looked contemptuously at the man in front of him.

"That is out of the question, of course," he said. "And that is not the point."

Berger appeared more confused than ever.

"What is the point?" he asked.

"To have courage, man! To have courage!"

"When it can lead to nothing?"

"Yes!"

The affirmative was delivered with heavy emphasis. But by that time Berger felt more calm, and he rejoined simply:

"Then courage may be stupid at times."

"What do you mean by that?"

The inquiry was sharp and curt, and the commissioner sat up straight in his chair.

"That it is stupid to risk one's life for the sake of seven thousand kroner. And I have a wife and a child."

Commissioner Lier smiled sceptically.

"Did you think of that?"

"It was the only thought in my mind."

"Then you were fully conscious of what you did? You were not panic-stricken? You were not at all startled and confused?"

The other man thought a while before he answered.

"Fully conscious?" he echoed pensively. "I shouldn't say that. But I was able to think. And that was the thought that came. And then I couldn't do anything except what I did."

"And you still think that you did right?"

"Yes, I still think that I did right. I still think that two hundred kroner is nothing to die for."

The commissioner gave a quick glance at the report.

"You said seven thousand a while ago?"

"Yes, that's right. I was thinking of Kvisthus now. He is the one who will die tonight for the sake of two hundred kroner." Then he smiled a hard and crooked smile. "I should have died for the sake of seven thousand."

The commissioner came back at him icily:

"Do you think this is something to make fun of?"

Berger had risen. As he stood there, his face was white and he looked utterly lost.

"I have not made fun of anything," he said. "One has every reason to wish that this had not happened to Kvisthus. He also had a wife and a baby."

"And does that matter when a man's most sacred duties are concerned? Do you really think it should matter?"

A pause ensued before Berger replied.

"Yes," he said. "Those two will have a hard time of it at any rate. And I believe that if he had had time to listen to them . . ."

He halted abruptly, his mind disturbed, his one desire to get out of it.

Something strange and ugly had come between those two men. The commissioner cut the interview short by rising and saying in a voice full of dejected resignation:

"That's enough. You don't understand what I mean anyhow."

3

WHEN Berger stood outside, in the light of the street lamp before the police station, and looked at the square and the streets, where cars rushed by and life went its accustomed way as if nothing had happened, he felt strangely empty and lethargic. He felt a pressure at his temples, and his ears were full of a vertiginous buzzing.

But he straightened up and tried to pull himself together.

"Did that man in there really mean what he said?" he asked himself in a state of perplexed wonderment. "Did he mean that I ought to be ashamed of not being dead now . . . that it was cowardly of me to let that fellow take only the money instead of letting him take both the money and my life?"

The fact that Commissioner Lier was a reserve officer struck him as an ameliorating circumstance. He did not go to the bottom of that thought. It merely flashed through him as he stood there pale and agitated.

It brought him a certain relief, however, and helped him to get along. It also occurred to him that he had better get home before they learned the news and became upset about him. This thought put some stamina into him, and he started off with a new decision.

To avoid meeting any one he knew, he chose streets with little traffic. His impressions were too fresh and too overwhelming to make it possible for him to stop and discuss them. But he tried to bring some order into it on his own account, and once more he lived through the entire incident . . . the suspense, the fear and panic that filled his mind before he formed his decision, the muddle in the street among a lot of incredulous faces.

"Yes," he thought, "I probably did look like a madman . . . bareheaded, coming out of a window, and carrying such news."

Then he recalled those two whom they had found inside when it was all over. And strange to say, the image of the discarded and emptied boxes had also burned itself into his memory. In particular he remembered the box of Kvisthus. It lay between two overturned stools and a mailbag. And it looked as if it had been thrown down with some force. One side of it was badly buckled and the lid hung sidewise by a single hinge. It was nothing but an ordinary tin box, green on the outside and red within. The tin tray with separate compartments for change and stamps lay beside it. And it was empty . . . yawningly empty. But the key still stuck in the lock.

The Leydersen's box had disappeared completely. At least, it had not been found when he left the office. Perhaps it was locked.

He recalled his own box, too. But . . . strange to say again . . . his memory of it was the vaguest. It stood undamaged and empty on a table.

"I suppose I should have thrown it on the floor before I ran for help," he thought in a fit of nervously ironic bitterness. "It would have looked more courageous, I guess."

But there he stopped himself.

"I must not sneer at him who must die. It was the box of Kvisthus that lay there. And he did show courage. At any rate, he did what I didn't. Maybe he had not time enough to think. If he had had that, he might have acted otherwise. Yes, I am sure he would. Good God . . . the way he looked!"

The memory of what he had seen sent a chill through him, and he had to close his eyes, while the upper part of his body was jerked backwards. His fists closed convulsively, and he walked more rapidly.

He was lying with his face against the floor . . . that dear, kindly Kvisthus. One arm was bent beneath his body while the other one was stretched out at a right angle. There were drops of blood in his thin, light hair . . . not very much . . . only a few drops. They were caused by a blow, probably. But it was another blow, or his fall against the stone slabs of the floor, that was going to kill him. For when they turned him over . . .

"O Lord, Lord!"

Berger groaned aloud as he walked along in a sort of daze, keeping to the middle of the street. He turned his head aside as if to escape something, and there was a choking sensation in his throat.

He strove to get rid of that impression by thinking of Lydersen. The red-headed fellow was sitting on the floor in a daze. When they came in, he jumped up with a kind of bewildered energy, as if he wanted to make a dash for something he couldn't quite make out. Later he made himself the center of the scene ... with Kvisthus. "We," he said repeatedly. "We ... we." And it was perfectly clear that he included no one but Kvisthus.

They had been taken to the hospital in the same car. But there was quite a difference between being killed and getting one's scalp scratched. One of them had lost his life, or was about to lose it, at least. The other one had lost nothing but a handful of red hair.

Berger worked himself into a state of subdued but intense bitterness. All of it was so typical of Lydersen ... a lazily dutiful time-server ... a light carefully placed on top of a bushel.

His was not a case to arouse sympathy. He would undoubtedly be paid with interest for that tuft of red hair.

Berger caught himself thinking ... and it was a thought he did not suppress: "I should care much less if it were Lydersen who had to die."

A FEW minutes later he reached his home. He rang his own door-bell with a sudden sense of profound depression. And the thought that bored into him while he stood there waiting was this:

"It might well have happened that I didn't stand here at all. It might have happened that I stood here for the last time when I came home for dinner."

This idea took such vivid hold of his mind that for a moment it seemed to represent reality. He saw himself stretched out on the floor dead. His face was chalky and his eyes glazed over. His hands were convulsively closed beneath his chin, which pointed upward in the rigor of death. Above his right eye was a dark hole with congealed blood around it, and from that eye, past the temple, ran a narrow ribbon of fresh blood which gathered in a viscid pool on the stone slab beneath his head.

Thus he saw himself . . . not one detail at a time . . . but in a single breath-taking, hallucinatory vision. He *knew* his own stocky figure as it lay thus . . . he knew his own face . . . those elongated, irregular features with the lean and too long nose at the center. Yes, he could even see the wart behind his right ear, just back of that dribble of blood.

In an agony of pain, with hard-set teeth and closed eyes, he leaned his distorted face against the doorpost while at the same time a realization of intense hunger caused his body to sag limply.

Then the door opened, revealing the frightened face of a child.

"Dad . . . are you sick?"

He straightened himself up and tried to smile, but it was a forced and pathetic smile.

"It's only my head . . . I have a slight headache . . . but it will pass when I have had some food."

He entered the hall, and the boy closed the door. The child was five years old. Now he stood watching attentively, while his father hung up his hat and coat.

"Mama is not at home."

Berger turned around quickly, disappointment showing plainly on his blanched face.

"Is she not at home?"

"No, but she'll soon be back. Fru Kvisthus asked her to come over and have coffee with her, and mama asked us not to eat until she got home. . . . But Dad . . . Daddy . . . what's the matter, Dad?"

Thoroughly scared, the boy tugged nervously at his father, who was leaning against the wall on the verge of collapse.

"What is the matter, Daddy?"

Then, by a violent exertion, Berger pulled himself together. Craving wildly for the intimate touch of something soft and living, he picked up the boy, put him on his shoulder, and carried him into the dining-room. He pressed his little body close to his own and said in a sorrowful tone:

"Kvisthus is dead, my boy."

The boy stared at his father, wide-eyed, disturbed, and surprised.

"Dead?" he wondered. "Dead?"

"Yes, my boy."

And his father looked back at him in dumb despair. He looked straight into the boy's face, now white as a sheet. Dejectedly he watched the stiffening of the boy's colorless lips. He saw his eyes brim over with tears in spite of an heroic effort to hold them back. At that moment he remembered, with a sense of pain, the toys which the jolly, child-loving Kvisthus always used to have on hand, and there was compassionate sympathy in the look he gave the boy, still perched on his shoulder.

But something entirely different was in the boy's mind. He buried his little hands in his father's long hair and pulled again and again with no thought of how it might hurt. And while he tried to smile, in order to show how brave he was, to show that after all he was a *big* boy, a cry of almost desperate joy broke from his lips:

"But you live, Daddy! You live, Daddy!"

A sense of happiness more profound than he had ever felt before swept through Berger. It filled him with a gratitude so boundless that it seemed almost religious.

"Are you glad of that?"

The boy slid down so that his head nestled against his father's neck and shoulder, and his little arms pulled their faces closer and closer together.

"Yes, Dad," he said. "Yes, Dad."

That was the moment when Berger grasped how tremendously lucky he had been.

HIS WIFE did not return until after nine. Berger and the boy had already had their supper. The boy having been put to bed, the man moved about the rooms in a state of restless nervous tension. Time and again he looked at his watch. When the door-bell rang at last and he went to open the door, his suspense had become almost unbearable.

It was she. Her face was white, but the red spots around her eyes showed that she had cried. She did not utter a word. All she did was to give him a long, questioning look. Then she entered the hall ahead of him.

Deep depression took hold of him as he watched her take off her coat, which he picked up and put in its wonted place. Still she did not say a word, but only sighed heavily. It was more like a moan. At last she stooped down to take off her rubbers, while he stood looking at her in the same helpless attitude.

When she was ready and erect again, they remained staring at each other in the dim light of the hall.

"Did you wait for me?"

"No . . . yes . . . that is to say. . . ."

The words wouldn't come. His lips trembled.

"I didn't think I could leave earlier. I wanted to wait until she came back from the hospital."

A tense expression came into his eyes.

"Did she go there? What did they say? Is he still alive?"

The last words were spoken in a very low, timid tone.

"Yes. But she didn't come back at all. They will let her spend the night there."

"And George?"

"Her mother came over. She will stay with the boy tonight. . . . Oh, the poor, poor child!"

Overwhelmed by her feelings, she buried her face in her hands and wept.

Berger felt absolutely lost, not knowing what to do or say. Nervously he rubbed and rubbed his hands, wet with perspiration, as he stood there looking at her. All the time something was struggling within him. And all of a sudden everything that had troubled him seemed to drop away . . . worry and distress, fear and suspense. Gently he let his hand glide over her hair.

After a while he said quietly:

"It might have been me."

Again he repeated his timid caress while deep stillness prevailed around them. Then she raised her face and gazed up at him with an intensity of pain in her expression that tore at his heart.

"Don't you know that I thought of that too?"

There was something like greed in his voice when he asked:

"Did you really?"

Impulsively he put his trembling hands about her tear-stained face . . . held it up against his own . . . stared into it searchingly, inquisitively, as if his very life were at stake.

"Yes, Erik!—Yes!—Perhaps you don't believe it, but I have been thanking God because it wasn't you. Don't you understand that?—Think only if it had been you! Think of me then! Think of our boy!"

It was as if a light had been extinguished within

him. His eyes fell. A sort of grieved hesitation appeared on his face.

"And think of me," he said tonelessly.

He shivered as if touched by a chill, turned around, and left her.

There was something pitiful about him that touched her conscience. She could always feel it, but today more than ever. She followed him softly, went up to him from behind, and put an arm around his bent and burdened neck.

"I didn't mean it that way," she said. "If you had been dead, that would have been worse than anything else, of course. You understand that, don't you?"

He nodded in silence. A little later he said:

"We have only one life."

LATER still Berger described briefly what had happened. Helen listened to him with a blanched face and wide-open eyes. When he was through, she went into the bedroom to kiss the boy good-night. She did this with a passionate, tormented fervor that almost waked the child. He grunted in his sleep, gritted his teeth a little, and turned over on his other side.

For a few minutes she stood looking down at him,

her eyes glistening with tears, her mind full of distress, full of sympathy for another little boy, but also full of an almost painful joy and gratitude to God because her own boy had escaped such a fate.

Then she returned to the dining-room, where Berger was walking up and down, restlessly, aimlessly, still upset. There she crouched on the divan. Covering herself with a shawl, she made herself as small as possible while, shivering with cold, she observed her husband walking slowly, endlessly from room to room.

She had been with Fru Kvisthus when the message came. Her own eyes and ears had taken in the effect of that message. And when she had kept still for about half an hour and had recovered her equilibrium somewhat, she was able to tell her husband about it.

Berger had pulled up one of the dining-room chairs and placed it with the back toward her. There he sat, straddling the chair and holding on to its back with both hands.

But he was not as deeply impressed by what she told him as he had expected. It did impress him . . . of course, it did . . . to hear about the despair and grief of those left behind. But personally he had faced something still worse, had been exposed to a much more profound impression. He had *seen*

Kvisthus . . . had seen the wounded and dying Kvisthus with his own eyes . . . had seen him lying on the floor, face downward, with the blood dripping through his bright yellow hair. And he had *seen* when they turned him over, when his crushed forehead became visible. . . .

For heaven's sake . . . it was Kvisthus who had to die, was it not? He was the one most closely concerned . . . at this time at least. Afterward the others would have to suffer also. But they were alive, even if they did suffer. And time would soften their suffering. But Kvisthus . . . it was he who had to die!

Berger had got on his feet again and was balancing the chair on two of its legs, swinging it back and forth. His face had turned white with excitement. His gray eyes were protruding. His dark, glossy hair was ruffled because he pushed one of his hands through it repeatedly.

Helen looked at him in surprise, almost with fear.

"What is the matter with you? Are you feeling sick? You should go to bed. This excitement has been too much for you."

He shook his pale, drawn face in energetic denial.

"Nothing is the matter with me except the fact that everything that you think most of is only of secondary importance. It is Kvisthus who was beaten.

It is he who must die tonight . . . who perhaps *is* dead by now. He is the one who has been wiped out. All of us are still alive. But he doesn't exist. This afternoon he still existed. We laughed and chatted together. And now he has ceased to be. He simply exists no longer."

She understood him, but she resisted on behalf of the others.

"No," she said, "but the others . . . they *do* exist. And think only what they have to go through. Can't you put yourself in their place?—Poor Kvisthus . . . I am so sorry for him! But he will die. He will suffer only this one night. And then think of those that are left behind. Think of what *they* have to suffer. Can't you see that?"

"Yes," he replied hoarsely. "Yes . . . but I can also see that it will pass. Little by little their suffering will become less acute. And I can see that they have days and days and years and years ahead of them . . . that they may still look forward to joy and happiness . . . that they will live to enjoy hours of laughter and fun . . . and that then their laughter will not be disturbed by a single little thought of him who is dead."

Then she asked him reproachfully and with a certain shrinking:

"Do you begrudge them that much?"

"No," he cried. "I don't begrudge them anything. But Kvisthus can look forward to nothing . . . not another day, not another laugh, not a smile, not a single happiness. He will never live again. That is what I am thinking of. That is what really matters."

With trembling hands, abruptly, he put the chair away, turned around, and drifted off.

He walked back and forth a couple of times, full of his burning thoughts. Then he began to look at her every time he passed by her. She sat as before, pale, curled up, and huddled beneath her shawl. And he looked and looked at her . . . pensively, shyly, moodily, and almost with fear.

Suddenly he stopped still and asked with insistent directness, as if there could be no difficulty about the answer:

"Do you love me?"

She started. Then she gazed at him in a frightened way as if trying to understand him. But she did not speak. And she did not understand.

"Do you love me, I asked. Can't you answer?—And answer you must if you care to have me go on living."

Then she began to understand. She put out her hand and pulled him wearily close to herself.

"Yes, Erik, I do!"

She burst into tears, her head pressed against his body. He stood up straight without looking at her. Without knowing what he was doing, he passed a finger softly across her neck, just above the hem of her blouse.

After a while he said quietly, as if it were enough to explain everything:

"If I had refused, I should have been dead now."

II

RINGS ON THE WATER

1

THEN a new day dawned. But it was not clean and unspotted, as most days are at the beginning. From the very start it had an ugly and troublesome aspect. Erik Berger was wide awake the moment he opened his eyes. He sat up in bed and discovered that Helen was not asleep either.

They regarded each other inquiringly, and Berger said:

"He is probably dead now."

Her eyes turned away as in fright. And he, too, had to look elsewhere.

As soon as he could get his clothes on, he went down to the floor below to use the telephone. When he returned, Helen knew at once what had happened ... that everything was over. Berger stopped inside the door and leaned against the wall.

"Yes," was all he said. "Yes ..."

But he must go to the office, and so he had to pull

himself together. They did not exchange a single word while eating breakfast. Several times Berger seemed to lose consciousness of where he was and forgot to eat. At last he gave up trying, rose from the table, put on his overcoat, gave Helen's hand a hard squeeze, and left without a word.

At the office all marks of the tragedy had been effaced, but the impression of it was strong in the minds of the men. Berger found his colleagues in groups, engaged in eager discussion. Even the men at the delivery windows were arguing about the incident with the people outside. All of this he could understand. It was quite natural. But why should they suddenly turn silent when he appeared? And why did they return his greetings in such a reserved manner?

"Perhaps I am that way myself," he thought.

Then the head of his division came up to him.

"The postmaster has asked for you. He wanted you to report to him as soon as you arrived."

Lydersen was already in the room. His head was bandaged, but otherwise he looked very much as usual . . . a little curt and sulky, that is, but perhaps somewhat more alive than under ordinary circumstances. His response to Berger's greeting was slightly embarrassed. Afterward he glanced speculatively at the postmaster, who was leaning back in his swivel chair, while one hand beat a tattoo on the desk in front of him. He was a man of about sixty-five, short, stocky, with the neck of an ox, and protruding ears. His clean-shaven face was stern and coarse.

He caught Lydersen's glance and gave in his turn a similar one to Berger.

"Well," he said at last, "suppose you sit down and explain yourself?"

Berger remained standing, utterly at a loss.

"Explain myself?"

"Yes . . . is there anything peculiar about that? You were in the battle, were you not . . . as an observer at least?"

The sarcasm of those last words caused Berger to start. He looked helplessly at Lydersen, on whose face he caught a faint, sneering grin. Then he blushed a vivid red. And at that moment a meaningless and until-then-forgotten detail came back to his mind . . . something that had happened at the police station.

It gave him the strength he needed for resistance.

"Yes," he said, "I was there as an observer. And it would have been better if Kvisthus also had been an observer."

The forehead of the postmaster turned an angry red . . . all the way up to the roots of his hair.

"Do you also mean to besmirch the man who is dead?" he asked. "I must say that you surprise me more and more."

Berger shook his head, taken aback by this unexpected turn.

"Besmirch?" he echoed. "Not at all . . . but I was his best friend. And all I am doing now is to wish that Kvisthus was not dead."

"Do you think yourself the only one who has that wish?"

"It sounds like it. If Kvisthus had done what I did, he would still be alive now. And it seems, on the other hand, as if I were at fault in being alive."

The postmaster hemmed with a show of consternation.

"I didn't mean my words to be taken in that way."

Berger stared at him in surprise.

"I am sorry if I misunderstood," he said. "How should they be taken?"

A momentary pause ensued. The postmaster stared back at Berger. There was disapproval, offense, and a suggestion of threat in his glance. Finally he remarked brusquely and decisively:

"We can come to that later. Just now I should

like to hear what you have to tell me. It might be interesting to find whether it tallies with Lydersen's story . . . which it must do, I am sure."

Berger related in few words what little he knew. His story was somewhat confused and jumbled. He told how he had been startled by Lydersen's outcry . . . how he had thought first of all of securing the money . . . how he had dropped this thought and rushed out to help when he heard a scream and the noise of a heavy fall. He told about the man with the gun and the mask that had been torn off . . . and of the final encounter with the second bandit.

"I had no choice," he said. "He would have taken the money under all circumstances, whether he had to shoot me or not. What was the use then of letting myself be killed?"

The postmaster pondered those words a little while.

"So you are quite sure that you could not have saved the money?"

"I am."

"Not even if you had tried a sudden attack on the man?"

Berger made a gesture toward his colleague with the bandaged head.

"You can see for yourself what happened to Lydersen."

"I do . . . but he made the attempt, nevertheless."

Berger nodded.

"Yes," he said, "I have thought of that, too. And I think it was stupid of him. He has every reason to feel happy at having escaped so easily. And the situations were quite different, for that matter."

"Oh, they were?"

There was confidence in the glance with which Berger appealed to Lydersen:

"Were they not?"

Lydersen looked back with wrinkled brow and an expression of disgust.

"I don't understand what you mean," he said. "Of course, I do understand that you have a certain interest in explaining away what happened . . . not only what happened to yourself, but to me. But I cannot see that your situation was any different from mine. And besides, you had more time to think."

Berger smiled rather arrogantly.

"Exactly," he said. "That was just what settled it. If you two had had a little more time, Kvisthus wouldn't be lying in a coffin today, and you wouldn't be wearing that decorative bandage."

Lydersen flushed violently.

"Decorative?" he asked angrily.

"That's the way it impresses me."

"No! No!"

The postmaster knocked warningly on the desk with the knuckle of his forefinger.

"No . . . I won't hear any more of that kind of thing. Personalities are entirely out of order. It is quite clear that your position in this matter is far less favorable than that of the others. They did their whole duty and a little more."

"And I?"

"Well . . . I can't say that you did your whole duty."

"Was it then my duty to die?"

"It was your duty to defend the money entrusted to your care."

"That's the same thing . . . as far as I can understand."

There was no reply from the other two.

"Am I right, or am I not?"

He turned first to Lydersen, who didn't move, but looked back at him with silent hatred. Then he turned to the postmaster.

"Am I right, or am I not?"

But the postmaster also evaded the answer.

"We won't discuss that now," he said. "You are too excited. And the answer is self-evident."

But Berger clung to that question of his. He would not permit it to be passed up . . . although he was fully aware of being over-excited. He wiped the perspiration from his forehead and tried to calm himself during the stillness that followed the postmaster's words. Standing there with downcast eyes, he managed at last to regain some self-control. When he looked up again, he was more composed. And he asked in a low voice, but insistently:

"This means then that the post-office department, which buys my services at a not very high price, demands that I shall risk my life when the money is at stake?"

The postmaster shook his head disapprovingly.

"Good Lord, no . . . no one *demands* such a thing of you. But the way you went about it has a very peculiar appearance. Even the police report makes mention of that fact."

He put his hand on some papers that were spread out on the desk before him.

"And that report will be forwarded to the department?"

"Yes . . . of course. But I don't think you are in danger of any charges or disciplinary measures.

There is nothing more to it than what I have said."

Berger straightened up, his face a little more colorless.

"That's enough," he said. "I have always tried to do my duty . . . and a little more. I have done as good work as any man in the office."

Unconsciously he made a movement of his head toward Lydersen, who met his glance with an embarrassed shrug of his shoulders.

"And," Berger went on, "I suppose it is the work I am paid for. I have sold my time, but not my life. And I feel happy and proud on account of what I did. I should do the same thing over again. Kvisthus was my best friend, but I have no desire to change places with him. I have no desire to be the corpse that is to be dropped out of sight with big words about faithfulness to duty. For that is not what really matters."

The postmaster looked at him with astonishment, and almost with a feeling of pity.

"What is it that matters then?"

Berger met the postmaster's glance firmly.

"That he is dead."

The postmaster rose, irritated and uncertain, and sauntered over to the window. When he turned back, a sort of patronizing pity had got the upper hand in his mind.

"You can take this afternoon off," he said. "You have been too badly upset to stay on duty. You may regard yourself as on sick leave."

The pale, sad face of Berger showed his painful surprise. Shaking his head firmly in refusal, he said:

"No, thank you. I am not sick, and I mean to go on with my work."

He turned abruptly to leave, but was stopped by Lydersen, who had risen in the meantime. He looked hurt as well as spiteful. The offense he had taken was evidently deep and fierce.

"Just one question," he said, "before you leave. There is one thing I should like to have cleared up in the presence of the postmaster . . . as he has heard everything else. What did you mean when you spoke of a difference in our situations?"

Berger stopped, comparatively calm.

"I have already explained that you were more taken by surprise."

"Was that all?"

"No . . . Did you hear that Kvisthus was being attacked outside?"

"Yes, of course."

"And did you know that it was an attack?"

Lydersen considered the question a moment.

"No," he replied evasively. "I didn't know it was an attack, but I knew something was wrong."

"Did you know that Kvisthus had been knocked down when the first man entered your room?"

"No."

"In other words, you didn't know how far anything was wrong?"

"I knew at any rate that I was facing a gun... I as well as you."

"But you didn't believe he would shoot?"

Lydersen gave a start. All of a sudden he looked foolish.

"How do you know that?"

"Because I heard what you said."

"What I said? I cried: 'Shoot if you dare!'"

A shadowy smile flickered over Berger's face.

"No, you didn't," he said.

Lydersen gazed at him in palpable confusion.

"Well, I'll be damned! Wasn't that what I cried out?"

"No."

While listening to them, the postmaster had become interested against his will. Now he bent quickly over the papers on the desk... just for a moment. Then he looked up.

"Yes, it was," he said decisively. "It is mentioned in the report."

Berger turned to the postmaster.

"Of course, it is," he said, "because that part of it was dictated by Lydersen himself."

A few seconds of uneasy silence followed. It was Lydersen who broke it.

"As you seem to know," he said, "what was it I cried?"

"You cried: 'You dare not shoot! You dare not shoot!' "

Lydersen blushed heavily.

"Are you sure of that?"

"I am. Because it meant a good deal. Of course, that other cry sounds a little braver besides. But I don't bother about that. If you care, you may assert privately that that was what you cried. It is not the point."

Lydersen looked as if he were trying to swallow something that wouldn't go down.

"Thank you," he said, "but . . ."

Then the postmaster asked a little impatiently:

"What is the meaning you have in mind?"

Berger's answer was directed to both of them, but he did not take his eyes off Lydersen.

"It is this," he said, "that the danger did not

look so very great to Lydersen. He did not believe that he was running any great risk. He did not believe that the man would shoot."

"And you did believe it?"

The question came from the postmaster.

With his eyes still fixed on Lydersen, Berger replied:

"I *knew* that he would."

"How could you know that?"

"First of all I heard the cry of Lydersen. It didn't suggest that lives were at stake. That's why I had time to think of the money. Then I heard the blow struck at Lydersen, heard his scream, and heard him fall. Then I knew that there was real danger outside. Finally I saw Lydersen lying on the floor, in front of the door, with a bleeding bandit bending down over him. *And I didn't know whether he was dead or alive.* Those are the three factors that make up the difference. And also the fact that I had more time to think. And then, perhaps . . ."

Berger hesitated and seemed to consider whether he should go on.

A glimmer of suspicion appeared in the glance with which Lydersen was watching him.

"And then, perhaps . . . ?" he urged.

"Well, I may as well say it, although it may offend

you. I don't think it will hurt you to hear it. What I had in mind was this: I am perhaps . . . no . . . I am certainly the most cold-blooded of us three, and I am not the more stupid of us two."

The rather inexpressive face of Lydersen flamed hotly.

"Thank you," he said in a choked and strained voice. "But I don't think you need to be worried about my stupidity."

"No, but I just had a desire to explain you . . . really explain you."

The lips of Lydersen twisted into a contemptuous smile.

"Explain what?" he demanded. "To whom?"

Berger gave him a hostile look.

"Yourself to yourself!" he replied harshly and fiercely.

2

THAT afternoon Berger stuck to his work with stubborn pertinacity. Little by little he managed to bear the curious glances thrown at him without taking them too seriously to heart. The early hours were the least busy during the entire day. Then he began to look for the evening papers. They appeared about four. The first thing that met his eyes was a two-column headline on the front page: "Post-office robbed by armed bandits." Then came other lines in smaller type: "One man killed and another beaten unconscious while trying to prevent the robbery. The bandits get away with 8,000 kroner."

With eyes that barely saw what he read, and with burning cheeks, he went on to what followed. The story itself was quite brief . . . as there was not very much to tell. His own name also appeared in it:

"Then they entered the money-order department. There they got the largest part of the plunder, and got it most easily, because the official in charge, Berger, who was alone at the time, deemed it wiser to give up the cash box without any resistance. There was at least 7,000 kroner in the box."

No trace had been found of those who committed the crime . . . nothing at all except that two men on a motor-cycle without a license number had been seen near the western limits of the city. They had also been noticed by two men a couple of miles beyond the city. After that they seemed to have sunk into the earth. No description of their appearance had been obtained because they were going at high speed and it was already growing dark.

Farther down on the same page another headline appeared: "The cycle found." This was the latest news: "After our main story had been printed, we learned from the police that the motor-cycle had been found in a ditch less than a mile from the city. It does not seem likely, therefore, that it was the robbers who were seen by two men farther out. It appears also that the cycle had been stolen in this city yesterday afternoon, probably just before the hold-up took place."

The principal editorial of that paper was also devoted to the crime. Having dwelt on the incredible, almost savage brutality shown by the robbers, and having tried to trace it to the spirit of the time, the writer went on to say: "In this connection two men deserve to be mentioned with the greatest respect, and one of them with deep sympathy, because his sense of duty cost him his life. The two officials we have in mind are Kvisthus and Lydersen. Both of them showed a heroism and a devotion to duty that call for public recognition in these degenerate days when the world seems to be ruled by cowardice and lawlessness. Kvisthus is dead, unfortunately, and nothing can be done except to deplore the loss of an able and popular official, and to wish that he may rest in peace. The other one, Herr Lydersen, must be kept in mind by the department. An adequate way of doing so can undoubtedly be found."

Berger didn't stir. The paper was spread out before him. He had sneaked in the reading of it while on duty at one of the money-order windows. Then his glance caught the death notices which appeared on the same page. In feverish suspense he ran his eyes down the column. There is was:

My dearly beloved husband,
and
My kind, devoted father,
ARNE KVISTHUS,
Was taken from us last night,
Aged Thirty-five.
ESTHER KVISTHUS. GEORGE.

This advertisement attracted him with hypnotic force. In an alarming, terror-inspiring fashion it bore witness to the fate of Kvisthus . . . that kindly, pleasant Kvisthus who would be seen by no one hereafter . . . by no one at all.

A subdued moan escaped Berger. Painfully he raised his eyes toward the window where Kvisthus used to sit, and where now one of the young men on probation was selling a stamp. His heart ached at the thought that Kvisthus should have been sitting there... that his hand should have received the money... that he should have passed out the stamp ... just that stamp. But the hands of Kvisthus would never be used again. They probably lay folded over his breast now. He "was taken from us last night, aged thirty-five."

The fate of that dead man sent a shivery chill through Berger. With unsteady hands he folded up the paper. Just then a woman appeared to get a money order, and he had to pull himself together. It was his plain duty to accept the money and to write out a receipt, giving name, address, and the sum paid in. That was his reason for being there. The office was the office.

But not a sound passed his lips.

AT LONG length that day also came to an end. When Berger rose to put his cash box into the safe, he could not help recalling the previous time he had done so. At that time Kvisthus was there. And the entire incident recurred to him, vividly, horribly.

"I was standing here," he thought in a state of great agitation. "There is the door I opened. Outside that door Lydersen was lying. But he was not dead after all. And then..."

No . . . he mustn't! He must pull himself together and get away from there. He was not going to remember that some one else was lying a little farther away.

"I must hurry home," he thought. "It is Saturday night, and they are waiting for me."

It was cold and clear outside, and it was already growing dark. A few stars appeared. And through his brain shot the thought that perhaps we had something to do with the stars when we died. Who could tell? Maybe we lived up there, looking down upon this earth with its joys and its misery.

"If you can see your loved ones from where you are now, then you will feel regretful tonight," he thought. "Then you will wish that you were here with us. With them. You also had a wife and a small boy. And they meant what they said about you in that advertisement. Oh, yes . . . they mean more than they said. But now, Arne, it is all over. Never will you have a chance to console them. Never will you be able to help them. You must stay where you are, even if they should cry loudly for you in dire distress. And that's what probably they are doing tonight. Perhaps you hear them calling. Perhaps you can see them. But you must stay where you are."

These thoughts made him dizzy. They caused him to feel very poor. They made the distance to heaven immeasurable, and they made life on earth seem bitter and futile.

"And yet," he thought, "all of us want to live. So do I, and so did he."

HELEN greeted him silently when he got home. It seemed to him that, somehow, she felt shy in his presence . . . that there was *something* in the air between them. He could not make out what it was, but it prevented him from getting away from his own painful thoughts.

When they were seated at the supper table, he asked with some astonishment and disappointment:

"Have you nothing good to eat tonight? It is Saturday . . . and I feel down in the mouth."

She hesitated a little.

"I forgot."

She tried to look at him . . . indifferently. But she could not manage it. Her glance slid away from him and rested on her plate.

Then, of a sudden, he saw her turn very pale.

"I didn't really forget it," she said slowly and with difficulty. "But I didn't think it was necessary . . . under the circumstances."

He felt strangely numbed and bewildered.

"Under the circumstances? What do you mean by that?"

She was still staring at her plate.

"Oh, nothing at all . . . nothing that is worth talking about."

And she began to eat in a peculiarly stiff and mechanical manner, as if she hoped that it might help her to forget.

Then he understood that she, too, had heard something. The blood rushed to his face. He sat absolutely still, staring at her, while she refused to meet his glance. A sense of deep disappointment seized him.

Then a small hand pulled at his sleeve.

"Aren't you going to eat, Daddy?"

It pulled him up. At that moment Helen raised her eyes and they looked searchingly at each other, as if they were trying to measure how deeply the other one had been hit. It lasted only a second. Then they looked away again.

But the boy smiled happily.

"You two are so funny," he said. "Why don't you eat?"

And they forced themselves to do what he asked. They also forced themselves to speak a few words, to talk nervously, with many pauses, about commonplace things. But all the time that *something* stayed achingly at the back of their minds.

When they left the table, Berger took the boy over to the divan. There they sat, prattling away about nothing at all, but it was good to feel a living being close to oneself. It was doubly good because that being was only five years old, full of trust, and very frank in his display of worshipping love... because that being was a child that knew nothing, understood nothing beyond the simple things of ordinary daily life.

His mother was in the kitchen, washing the dishes. At nine o'clock she came in to help the boy take his Saturday bath before going to bed.

The little one could feel that something had happened. It was made clear to him by his mother's reserve and by the tenderness of his father while they sat together on the divan. Now he looked up at his mother with a pleadingly pleasant and yet sad smile.

"I can wash myself," he said. "Come and sit down here and be nice to Daddy."

But she carried him away without replying... firmly, but without any sign of disapproval. And the boy went along in obedient resignation.

Berger lighted his pipe and began to walk about while waiting for those two to get through. He guessed that there was more to come. And it troubled him to have to wait for it.

First the boy came into say good-night, and to be carried back to his little bed. He took a great pleasure in this function. It was one of the big moments of every day. And he wouldn't miss it that night either. The father did his part in his usual gay and smiling fashion.

Then Berger resumed his walk through the other rooms. When Helen came in and sat down with a piece of sewing, he knew that something was about to happen. But it was a long time before she spoke. He had sat down, too, a little embarrassed, his hands behind his head, the chair tilted against the wall. Thus he watched her. There were no outward signs to go by. She looked much as usual. Perhaps there wasn't anything after all... or nothing but a slight attack of bad temper... or something that she had already put out of her mind.

Then he gave a start, but so slight a one that it hardly showed. He seemed to be watching her quietly as he had done all the time. She had merely raised her eyes to give him a scrutinizing glance. And he had understood that there was something

...after all...something against which she had been fighting.

Then the blood suddenly left her face again. Dark rings of fear appeared around her eyes. And she asked...directly, without a word of introduction:

"Have you seen the paper?"

He remained quiet outwardly, constrained as before.

"Yes. Have you?"

"Yes," she answered curtly.

Once more it looked as if the thing had passed over.

But after a while she said:

"They have a lot of nice things to say about Kvisthus and Lydersen."

"Yes," he assented.

When she went on sewing and nothing more was said, he rose nervously. Just then she looked up at him. Her face was pale again, and he noticed the shadows around her eyes.

"They have nothing to say about you," she remarked. "Neither good nor bad."

"No," he said.

Then he left her, walked back and forth a few times, nursed her words in his mind, and suffered from them. His steps were more rapid than before, more restless, more disturbed. Suddenly he stopped, picked up the paper from the table, and went close to her. His hands trembled when he opened the paper and spread before her the page with the editorial and the death notice. He was paler than she, and his voice almost broke from excited disappointment as he pointed to the different items on that page and asked:

"If you are to be perfectly honest, do you really think that what you see down there is worth what appears up there? Do you think that the praise is worth the price?"

She rose instinctively. They stood very close together. Her lips began to quiver as she stood there watching the infinite loneliness of his disappointment.

"No," she said. "No!"

It was as if something had snapped within her. She leaned her head against his shoulder and wept.

Full of embarrassed gratitude, he patted her hair. It was as if he had won her back from something that was foreign and hostile.

Then she raised her head. An expression of almost painful hardness was on her tear-stained face.

She took hold of his arms so fiercely that it hurt him, and then she said:

"Can't you understand? I love you so much that I cannot bear to have anybody speak badly of you."

He was pale again, and looking down at her, he again felt lonely as before.

"Has anybody done that?"

"Yes," she replied in a hard voice.

Once more something seemed to snap within her. Again she clung to his shoulder, sobbing so that her whole body shook.

He caressed her head absent-mindedly and said in a low, muffled tone . . . as if he were disposing of it once for all:

"It does not matter."

But his face had stiffened strangely.

3

THE next day, Sunday, neither one of them went out. There was no agreement to that effect between them. They just let it happen that way. And they felt better on that account . . . considering the circumstances.

When Monday morning came, gray and commonplace, Berger was summoned to the police station for another examination. It astonished him somewhat. And it angered him too. His recollections of the first examination were still painfully fresh. But without protest he gave up his post at the window to another man and went to meet whatever was in store.

At the police station he told them who he was and noticed that his appearance caused a certain stir. The officer at the desk was nervously eager to show him the way to the commissioner's office.

The commissioner was ready and had evidently been waiting for his arrival.

"Sit down," he said. "There are just a few questions I wish to have answered in addition to your earlier statement."

His hands seemed restless as they played with a written sheet that was lying on the desk in front of him. It even seemed as if he hesitated.

Berger seated himself with a sense of comparative safety. He had told everything he had to tell that first evening. After he was seated, he had time to look around while waiting for the commissioner to begin. He noticed that the October sun lighted a column of dust right across the room, ending finally in a brighter spot that exactly covered the papers lying on Commissioner Lier's desk. It reminded Berger of the spotlight in a theatre.

"Yes," he thought, "I suppose those are the papers that will play the main part by and by. I guess there have been no arrests as yet."

But the continued silence of the commissioner disturbed him at last, and he began to wait with that aching impatience that seizes us when we know ourselves faced by something unpleasant and are anxious to get through with it.

He was badly startled when the commissioner cleared his throat. He watched intently as he saw that huge bulk of flesh with the unprepossessing face bend over the papers. He followed the movements of the man's fishlike eyes as they passed down the lines, and he had a feeling that everything depended on what those eyes found in those lines.

"Then you actually saw both robbers?"

Again Berger gave a start.

"Yes," he answered. "But, of course, the whole thing lasted only a couple of minutes."

Lier was leaning forward, his arms resting on the desk, his eyes glued to Berger.

"Then you didn't recognize them?"

Berger shook his head.

"No," he replied. "And the one of whom I had the best view had his face covered by a black mask."

"What kind of a mask? Can you remember?"

"No, the only thing I can remember is that it was black."

"Was he tall or short?"

"Rather tall, I should say. And I think I have said so before."

The commissioner glanced at the papers again.

"Yes," he said, "that's right. So that is one thing you remember?"

"Yes."

Another pause occurred. With uneasy impatience Berger waited to have it broken. But it took time. At last the commissioner straightened up so that only his wrists rested on the table. He looked openly interested as he said:

"Then there was the other one . . . he who did not wear a mask."

A momentary sense of surprise made Berger's face appear boyish and somewhat confused.

"Yes," he said, "but I have told all I know about him also."

"Absolutely everything?"

"Yes . . . I think so . . . I don't know. . . ."

He was conscious of his own sense of growing confusion, but he found himself unable to check it.

The gaze of the commissioner rested firmly on him.

"Absolutely everything?"

"Yes, of course . . . I don't know anything more . . . I had a mere glimpse of the man."

"But he had no mask?"

"No . . . that is . . . there was a black rag hanging beneath his chin."

"But it did not cover his face?"

"No."

"And you didn't recognize him?"

Berger shook his head regretfully.

"No, I didn't recognize him."

The commissioner leaned back in his chair. He put his right hand over his stomach, with the thumb between two waistcoat buttons. The other fingers of that hand were drumming nervously.

"No, you didn't," he said. "You didn't."

He looked almost as if he were falling asleep. A moment later he raised his head and asked in a casual way:

"How old do you think they were?"

Berger thought a good deal before he answered.

"It's hard to tell. But I should say that they

were between thirty-five and forty . . . probably more nearly forty."

"In other words, about your own age."

The comparison made Berger squirm.

"Yes," he admitted.

Then the commissioner leaned forward again, put his arms on the desk, and looked him straight in the eyes, firmly, insistently.

"And you are *quite sure* that you didn't recognize them?"

Berger's pale, drawn, and suffering face turned a flaming red. But he didnt move, and there followed a minute of dreadful silence.

"You don't answer?"

Berger knotted his forehead defiantly.

"I have answered," he said. "But I know what you mean."

"What do I mean?"

"That I am implicated in the crime."

The commissioner raised his eyebrows.

"It is you who say that," he rejoined casually.

"Yes, but you put the words in my mouth. And I should like to know at once: Is there a charge against me . . . or is there not?"

The other man hesitated, evidently feezed by the situation.

"A charge?" he repeated. "No . . . not in the proper sense. But here we are. We know nothing. We have nothing to take hold of. For this reason we are forced to grope our way ahead. We have to consider every possibility, even if, unfortunately, we should have to hurt some one's feelings."

Berger's face twitched slightly.

"Some one's?" he said, deeply disturbed. "That's me, of course?"

That repressed sense of revolt seemed about to choke him. His throat felt strangely contracted, and he could barely speak.

The commissioner rose.

"For the moment it is," he said. "And you will have to bear with it. I don't find your implication likely or reasonable. But on the other hand there are circumstances which suggest that the criminals possessed some knowledge of the arrangements. And to this must be added your own attitude of complete indifference."

Berger's face was pale and frowning while he listened to those words.

"Is that the reason?" he asked in a low voice.

The commissioner gave him a quite human look, touched by his tone.

"Yes, that's the reason," he said. "That, and

nothing else. You have no cause to suspect anything more than that. And the office gives you a very high character. But nevertheless you must admit that it is peculiar . . . extremely peculiar . . . that in spite of your evident sense of duty, you should surrender the money without the least effort at resistance."

Berger's mind became filled with a sense of resigned weariness, apathetic placidity. And he asked in a strangely timid and injured tone:

"In other words, I should have let myself be shot?"

The commissioner shook his head impatiently.

"Why must you push the matter to that extreme? There is no reason to think that he would have had the courage to shoot, if *you* had displayed any courage at all."

Then Berger looked up at him, goaded into instinctive resistance.

"You were not there," he said firmly. "You don't know just how it happened."

"Well, explain yourself . . . you who were there."

Berger shook his head.

"It can't be explained."

With a shrug of his shoulders, as if he gave it all up, the commissioner turned away from him and began to walk back and forth in front of the desk.

Berger sat still, buried in his own thoughts. Something had happened to him that he had never thought could possibly happen . . . something that shook the foundations of his being and paralyzed his will power.

After a while the commissioner came to a halt right in front of him.

"Have you talked with anybody since it happened?"

Berger had to make an effort to answer.

"Not except here, in the office, and at home."

"Not even yesterday, which was Sunday?"

"No, I was at home the whole day."

"And you can prove that?"

"Yes, my wife was also at home."

"You say that a little uncertainly?"

There was a plea in Berger's eyes . . . a shy and timid plea.

"No," he said. "It is the truth. But I shouldn't like you to ask her . . . to let her know. . . ."

He had to stop, and his eyes fell.

"What has happened here?"

"Yes, that's it."

The commissioner stood looking at him, and there was pity in his glance. A moment later he asked:

"Have you many friends?"

Berger shook his head.

"No one that is very close to you?"

Then Berger looked up.

"Not now, when Kvisthus is dead."

"He was then a *very* close friend of yours?"

"Yes."

Once more the commissioner seemed to consider, but this time face to face with Berger.

"Well," he said at last, "then there is nothing more I have to ask you. Thanks."

Berger rose slowly and looked suspiciously at the other one. For a moment he seemed incapable of believing that his ordeal was ended.

Then the commissioner said:

"There is no reason why you should take this so much to heart. No one will know about it. And it has no particular significance. You must understand that we have to try all possible lines... whether they seem probable or not."

Berger was unable to reply. He saluted silently and left... relieved to have it all over.

Not until he stood in the street, alone again and in broad daylight, could he fully grasp the desperate ruthlessness of the insult to which he had been exposed. He was on the verge of screaming out his sense of agonized rebellion. They had taken him for a thief . . . for a thief capable of committing murder. They had at least considered the possibility of his being such a man!

"If only no one finds it out!" he thought nervously, his mind sickening with a tormenting sense of mortification. "Helen, at least, must never know about it. She is too much upset already, and she will never be able to understand."

But he must pull himself together. He must return to the office as if nothing had happened. No one would dare to ask him any questions, not even if they had any suspicions. They would look at him, of course, and try to read his face. But that had to be borne. That would be his punishment for having preserved his life without special permission.

"That's the way it looks," he thought. "It looks as if it had made me a criminal . . . or at least a man that others can look down on."

Just then the thought of Kvisthus came back to him. He had to stop in order to consider that alternate possibility.

"Would you change?" he asked himself.

He repudiated the thought with a shake of his head.

"And if Kvisthus had the chance . . . knowing everything . . . do you think *he* would change?"

Without the least hesitation he was able to reply:

"Indeed, he would. I am alive at any rate. I am standing here on the street. I *am*. And we live only this once. He will never be permitted to come back."

But as he walked on, he was again overcome by that sudden anxious feeling of shame. So that was how a person felt when innocently accused . . . when he became a marked man in the eyes of other men!

Then his mind turned strangely, stubbornly callous. As he walked down the street, he was not aware of the life stirring around him. He was only aware of his own inner life, and he felt it as an ache, a torment . . . but also as a pulsing, breathing mercy . . . in spite of all.

AT THE office everything was as usual . . . dark, gloomy, commonplace, and unchangeable. Those rooms did not look as if they had ever been the scene of a tragedy.

With a nod which he made as casual as possible, he relieved the man who had filled his place and took over the window himself. There was business at once. And then more of it.

But while he worked, mechanically, as if his real

self had not been a part of it, a sense of revolt began to take shape within him . . . a desperate, acrimonious tendency to resist . . . a self-defensive hatred which seemed to excite and consume him because it could find no definite objective.

"No, no!" his mind hammered away. "I'll be damned if I can stand it any longer. I'll drop everything and walk out!"

But he knew that it couldn't be done, and so he remained sitting where he was.

A little later he discovered suddenly that he was on his feet, and he heard his own voice . . . stiff and toneless . . . saying to the assistant postmaster, who occupied the same room:

"Please keep an eye on the window here. I want to see the postmaster for a moment."

He left without waiting for an answer. And all the time he had a feeling of being some other person . . . some one who merely acted on his behalf.

The postmaster looked up inquiringly and saw before him a face that was as white as that of a corpse and that looked back at him inquiringly.

"Do you know that the police have tried to charge me with being an accomplice in the robbery?"

The postmaster looked away in evident discomfort.

"Yes," he replied finally.

"Is there any one else here who knows?"

"No . . . and no one will know about it."

Berger stood looking at that head bending over the desk.

"Do you really believe that?"

A brief pause followed. Then the head was raised.

"No," the postmaster answered, firmly and quietly.

They looked at each other embarrassedly . . . for something like a whole minute. Then Berger turned and walked out.

He walked past the assistant postmaster, past the cash box, on to the toilet. There he leaned helplessly against the wall and broke into convulsive sobbing.

4

KVISTHUS was buried at half past one on Wednesday afternoon. The group of mourners was quite a large one, but the host of curious onlookers was larger by far. They formed numerous knots between the gates and the chapel, and they pushed offensively close. Those who could not find a place on the walks trampled on the graves. Most of them were women.

Remarks were made freely about the more notable persons passing in review. Apart from the widow and son, there were two people who attracted special attention. They were Berger and Lydersen.

Lydersen walked by himself, reserved and dignified, with the bandage showing beneath his hat. He was well aware of the attention paid to him, and for this reason he walked very slowly, looking straight ahead.

Berger walked with Helen. They walked rapidly, as if wishing to get under cover as quickly as possible. Once Berger tried to speak in order to appear unconcerned. His only response was a despairing glance out of a pale face, and he gave up in bitter resignation.

"If she could only take it a little more sensibly," he thought, "then it would be much less difficult to endure."

They exchanged no greetings in the chapel, but sought a place for themselves in one of the rearmost pews. From there they could just get a glimpse of Fru Kvisthus and George, who were seated with other members of the family. Both of them were startled by the sight of Esther. It was as if the whole thing came closer to themselves as they watched the drooping figure of that young woman, weeping behind her black gloves. The boy was seated beside her, white and rigid. Although they had imagined the scene just like that . . . although they had known that it would be like that . . . the actual vision of it affected them vividly, as if it had been a complete surprise.

Moved by a sudden sense of distress, Helen put her hand within Berger's arm and huddled against him in a spell of agonized grief that caused her whole body to shiver. Tears came dripping down her face, and she squeezed the arm of her husband harder and harder.

It filled him with a feeling of warm tenderness. A process of softening began within him. A craving for understanding which had been suppressed for several days now had a chance to assert itself. Cautiously, gratefully, gently, he stroked her hand. And she pressed closer to him, stirred by helpless resentment.

When a hymn had been sung, the minister spoke with deep emotion.

"We are a great host of mourners," he said, "we

who have come here to join the wife and the little son of the dead man. And it is natural that we should ask: O Lord, *must* such a thing happen? Was it necessary? Would it not have been possible that he remained alive among us? We needed his smile, O Lord, and we needed his kindliness. Why, O Lord, should his young wife suddenly, unexpectedly be left without a protector, guide, and friend? Why should his son have to grow up without the father whom he will miss bitterly?

"Yes . . . such are the questions which we human beings ask. But the wisdom of God is hidden from us. We do not know what He has meant by this. We cannot know the purpose for which the deceased may have been reserved. Jesus Himself said: Now thou canst not understand what I am doing with thee, but a time will come when thou shalt understand.

"The time will also come when Kvisthus will understand. Some time he will learn that it was necessary . . . that it was for his own good.

"And one thing we know. We know how he died. We know that he died honorably at the post where God had placed him. He did not hesitate when duty called on him to risk his life. He did the only thing that is natural and right for a loyal and self-respecting man to do: He defended his post. He staked his life . . . and lost it."

The minister said a great deal more, but Berger did not listen to it. Something had happened to him again, and he felt more helpless, more poverty-stricken than when he came.

During the first part of the address, Helen continued her frightened squeezing of his arm. But when the minister spoke about the death of Kvisthus, Berger could feel her grip loosening and weakening. At last she freed her hand cautiously and let it drop limply into her lap.

Berger's face remained immovable. He did not try to see where the hand went. He sat there rigid and motionless and let it happen, while his eyes were turned steadily toward the minister. But the words no longer reached him. He was outside the whole thing. He was nowhere.

What brought him back to consciousness was the sudden sound of violent crying. Then he could turn his face, and he saw Esther Kvisthus stooping deeply and weeping wildly into a handkerchief held between her black-gloved hands. Her whole figure, girlishly slender, was shaken by convulsive, uncontrollable sobs.

From that moment he could not take his eyes

off her. He saw that she could barely keep her seat ... that her despair had made her almost unconscious ... that she heard nothing, knew nothing of what was going on around her. Neither he nor she had any impression of the hymn that followed, or of the placing of the wreaths on the coffin.

Then the coffin was carried out to the grave. Berger and Helen walked side by side like two strangers. Her eyes were cast down. Her face was drawn but inscrutable. Something crashed within him. He felt more calm, but also more bitter. It seemed all of a sudden as if that dead man in front was the real enemy ... the main cause of all the evil with which Berger had been deluged.

When the coffin was being lowered, Fru Kvisthus broke down again. She wept loudly and wailingly while she pressed the boy close to herself. When the minister had cast earth on the coffin, she grew more composed. Together with the boy she let herself be led up on the boards that covered the piles of earth surrounding the grave. There she stood, a strangely lonesome and deserted figure, staring down into the hole where they had put him.

Mechanically she received the condolences... without looking at those that passed before her, or at least without recognizing them.

The Bergers also went up to her. Helen went first. Then Fru Kvisthus seemed to wake up. All at once she was able to see. Questioningly, despairingly she looked at the other woman, until the latter had to lower her eyes.

Then Berger stepped forward with bared head and out-stretched hand. And then something happened. She grabbed his hand between both of hers and raised her tormented face toward his while the tears streamed down her cheeks.

"Oh, Erik," she burst out, "why didn't he do as you did?"

And suddenly she dropped her head against his shoulder and wept like a child.

It was over in a moment. But it was as if she had sought protection . . . or understanding . . . or peace . . . or help.

THIS INCIDENT rendered Berger more confused and helpless than ever. On the way home, he and Helen remained silent. They did not have the courage to look at each other.

"Is she offended?" he wondered.

The thought of Esther Kvisthus stirred him deeply. He saw her vividly, as in a dream . . . saw her as she sat in the chapel, bent far forward . . .

saw her standing beside the grave and looking first at Helen, then at himself.

And he heard the words that broke from her lips ... words that did not reproach him, Berger, but the other one:

"Why didn't he do as you did?"

She was the first and only human being who had spoken to him like that. But then, she was the only one who knew what those words implied ... who was aware of all the horror with which they were fraught.

After they had reached their home, and when Helen persisted in her attitude of silent and sullen offense, those words pursued him like a stimulating and redeeming expression of mercy.

THE EVENING paper carried a long story about the funeral. Both of them read it, but neither one spoke of it. In fact, they did not at all refer to what had happened.

Not until the next evening.

The moment Berger got home, he knew that something was up. It was something that reminded him of the preceding Saturday. It made him nervous, but he asked no questions. All the time at the supper table he waited for it to break loose ...

waited in a state of fright . . . for he knew, or at least suspected, what it was.

Suddenly she looked up, her face white with anger. She could hold it back no longer.

"Did you see that Esther has received one thousand kroner from the government, and that Lydersen has been granted a reward . . . a complimentary reward! . . . of five hundred kroner?"

He nodded.

"Yes," he replied timidly. "But you will do me a favor by not talking about it."

There was challenge in her attitude.

"Why not? I think you will have to bear with my talking about it."

"Suit yourself," he answered wearily.

There was something in his tone that silenced her . . . a suggestion of a burdensome weight too heavy to be borne much longer. But an evil spirit was still at work within her and pressed for utterance. It was difficult to hold back. She suffered in the attempt . . . just as she suffered at the thought of having to let it out sooner or later.

Berger left the table early and with nothing but a silent nod. He had no sooner begun a restless and agitated wandering about the rooms than Leif came up to him. The boy looked at his father with anxious surprise.

"Are you sick again, Daddy?"

Berger stopped and tried to swallow the pain that clutched at his throat.

"No," he said gently. "Why do you ask?"

"Because you looked so funny."

The father smiled, but the weariness of that smile did not escape the child. Intuitively the boy felt that consolation was needed. And he seemed bent on creating a diversion as he took hold of his father's hand.

"Come along and I'll show you something."

At that moment his mother appeared in the doorway.

"You must go to bed," she said brusquely.

The boy looked regretfully at his father and tried bravely to smile in order to cheer him up, but the smile was crushed. Then he went off to bed. A few moments later he returned in his nightshirt to say good-night. It was a long story, ending with the customary ceremony. At last the light was turned out in the bedroom. But the door was allowed to remain open.

Half an hour later Helen came in and sat down to read the papers. Berger continued his slow, pensive walk around the table. He noticed that the first thing she looked for was the notice about Lydersen, and it brought a faint smile to his face . . . a fatigued and indulgent smile.

Just then she looked up.

"Are you smiling at me?"

He shook his head in an effort to propitiate her.

"No, at everything and everybody."

To this remark she gave no answer. Once more she gave the paper a brief glance. Then she folded it up and put it away, saying with a sigh of acrid disappointment:

"Oh, yes . . . some people reap honor . . . and others reap shame."

Then he stopped to look at her. The table was between them.

"Will you never learn to see this matter rightly?"

Without looking at him, she answered:

"I can only see one thing . . . that it is dreadful to be dishonored. It maddens me to see an idiot like Lydersen . . . who always, *always,* has been far behind you . . . suddenly get so far ahead of you that you never can catch up with him again."

"So you really care for my honor?"

She looked up, her eyes on fire, her face still pale.

"I do! And I can't understand this. I can't understand that just you . . . you who have always been so devoted to your duty . . ."

She laughed a bitter, scornful laugh:

"To give up the money! You might have done *something.*"

Outwardly he remained self-possessed. But his thin, irregular face showed an injured expression, from which, with a sort of voluptuous horror, she gathered that her blow had gone home. And she waited for his reply.

"Yes," he said, "I might have raised an arm."

The hardness of her expression changed into one of bewilderment. She gazed uncomprehendingly at him. Then she asked unsteadily:

"Yes, why didn't you do that?"

"No," he answered, "I didn't think it worth while to use it for that purpose alone."

"Not worth while?"

"No, not in comparison with the use I could make of it later, if I kept still then."

He turned around and resumed his walk. But there was more on her mind. The lack of color in her face showed him that something was fermenting within her . . . something of which she was ashamed, and which nevertheless she could not hold back.

Yet he was taken by surprise when she finally spoke.

"You are good at making excuses," she said. "And then there was that scene at the grave yesterday. There you were, making a spectacle of yourself, and I had to stand by, looking like an idiot. And everybody was taking it in. Just as if they hadn't had their full of staring at us in the chapel. Oh, it just made me boil!"

His face had turned scarlet. And he demanded harshly:

"Was that my fault?"

When she did not reply, he added sarcastically:

"You were softer . . . you took it quite differently . . . that night when you came home after having seen her. But then you didn't know yet that I had some enemies with whom you could join hands."

He paused a moment.

"There is something else I must tell you. If I had been dead, you would have made just as much of a scene as did Esther Kvisthus, if not more. And if Kvisthus had done what I did, you would have said to him . . . or at least you would have thought: Oh, Arne, why didn't he do as you did?"

"And I suppose she would have done to him what I have done to you?"

"Yes," he answered, "you are no worse than the rest."

Then she rose and put away the chair as if to leave. But as she was pushing the chair under the table, that agitation which she had vainly tried to control forced her to say:

"Perhaps you are right. But nevertheless she has been spared certain things that I have to stand. Do you know what happened to your son this afternoon . . . just before you came home? He came in crying. And when I asked what was the matter, he said that the other boys had told him that his father was a good-for-nothing coward."

He saw that she regretted her words the moment they were spoken. And he could feel the blood receding from his own face. Unable to answer, he stood there, leaning with trembling hands against the top of the table.

Then they heard a commotion in the bedroom, and in the next moment the boy appeared in the doorway, excited and crying.

"For shame, mama!" he said. "For shame! You promised me not to tell. You promised me . . ."

He seemed so heart-breakingly overwhelmed that a warm feeling began to steal into his father's heart. Without looking at his wife, Berger went over to the boy and picked him up in his arms, in order to carry him back to bed.

The boy threw his arms impulsively around his neck.

"Yes, she did, Daddy!"

"All right, my boy. Don't cry now. It doesn't matter."

He patted the boy's back reassuringly and carried him off, feeling rich and happy in spite of everything.

In the darkened bedroom a wet cheek was laid consolingly against his own. And he was held back by two little arms after he had put the boy into his bed.

"Daddy," he heard the boy whisper, "you mustn't mind."

And a moment later he heard him say:

"I am so glad."

He patted the little one again.

"Why are you glad?" he asked.

"Because you let them take the money.... I would rather have you."

Berger gave the child's damp little hand a firm squeeze. Then he straightened up, said good-night once more, and went back to the dining-room.

Helen stood there looking at him, hard and locked up within herself.

Then he went over to her, very close, and said more firmly than he had ever spoken before:

"You said that I could have done *something*. Yes, I could. I could have made *him* fatherless, *you* a widow, and *myself* a corpse."

When she did not respond, but merely bit her lip, he went on:

"Now I am going out. But before I go, I want to tell you one thing. You had better put a stop to this kind of thing. I don't ask you to realize ever that I did the only thing that was right . . . for your sake, but most of all for my own sake. I merely ask you to stop . . . to permit me to live my miserable, worthless life in peace. Good-night."

For hours Berger walked and walked through the lonely evening. He passed the poor quarter on the outskirts of the city and reached a country road. No clear thoughts tormented his mind, but his whole being was saturated with a sense of resentment and isolation.

He longed for other human beings, for life. It pained him to find himself suddenly, unexpectedly placed apart from the rest. It shocked him and made him bitter.

It was after midnight when he came home. Helen was in bed, but awake. When he also had gone to bed and turned out the light, she sidled over to him, remorseful and unhappy. She patted his cheeks over and over again, and he could feel her tears dropping down on his face.

"Forgive me," she said at last. "I couldn't keep it back. I know that it was cruel of me, but I have had such a hard time."

He accepted her overtures with the humble joy of the outcast who meets an out-stretched hand. He accepted them, even though he guessed that the hand soon would be withdrawn again.

5

WHAT had hit Lydersen hardest during that discussion in the postmaster's office was neither Berger's reference to his lower intelligence nor the assertion that he was less cold-blooded. Both allegations were offensive enough. But they could be regarded as the expressions of a momentary excitement, of a lack of mental balance caused by the tragedy.

What really had hit him was the insinuation that

his bandage was decorative. There was personal animus in that suggestion. It was a barbed arrow that could not be disregarded. It proved that Berger had been angered by that visible evidence of Lydersen's greater courage. It also proved Berger's opinion that he, Lydersen, was making too much of a display of that evidence. It had almost sounded as if Berger thought him vain of his appearance and ready to use it for public effect.

This went home. It was a piece of malicious and vindictive meanness. It was like putting dirt in a wound.

But when dirt gets into a wound, the white corpuscles rush forth and help to eliminate it. That is just what happened in the case of Lydersen. All his repressed dislike of Berger, all the stored-up bile of a less able colleague, now rushed forth and produced a contemptuous hatred against Berger. Who was he anyhow, and what kind of delusions did he have about himself? Had he not in the hour of danger showed himself a cowardly poltroon, timid as a rabbit? Was he a person to whom one need pay any attention at all?

But the gathering of the white corpuscles to attack the dirt is accompanied by pain. This was also what happened in the case of Lydersen. His vanity smarted and ached. It was like a boil on his personality. And that boil had to be lanced.

Nothing was so insignificant that it could not be used against Berger. He pursued the same policy with the postmaster, with their colleagues, and in every talk he had with the police. He used no big words, indulged in no open denunciations. But he dropped little contemptuous side-remarks which, taken each one by itself, were no more damaging than so many shoulder-shrugs. But little by little they turned into drops that wore a hole in the stone.

Of all this he was not clearly conscious. But he kept on doing it, instinctively, without any thought of what he did.

During the entire week he did not speak to Berger ... not one single word. But whenever he passed him, he looked at him with an expression of profoundly reproachful disdain.

"He had better not get any fool notions into his head," Lydersen thought. "Perhaps he does show a little more practical ability than I do. So he likes to think anyhow. But we'll see. Perhaps other qualities will also be considered in the long run. It's of no use for him any longer to feel so very uppish."

LYDERSEN lived in a better-class boarding-house.

The other boarders were a couple of female teachers, the proprietress of a small handicrafts shop, several engineers, a bank teller, and an assessor of taxes. There were some ten or eleven of them, and they always moved in groups. The ladies formed one group, the engineers another, while the teller and the assessor constituted a somewhat looser combination, and the fourth group was formed by Lydersen alone.

During the three years he had lived in that place, he had had little or no intercourse with the other groups. At the table he partook in the perfunctory conversation without any special enthusiasm, in his own somewhat brusque manner. And once in a while he would enter the living-room during an evening, when, for instance, the programs at the film theatres were unusually poor or the weather was so bad that he did not care to venture out.

This is exactly what happened the Sunday after the funeral of Kvisthus.

The ladies were seated in and around the sofa, talking in subdued voices about a game of solitaire. Engelhardt, the engineer, was reading a detective novel. Lydersen drifted here and there aimlessly, while Rognaas, the bank teller, was improvising nervously on a piano that had not been properly tuned.

Lydersen felt somewhat depressed, suffering the after-effects of a too-intoxicating week, during which he had found himself the centre of public attention. Now his life was about to drop back into its accustomed monotony. No one had asked him a single question during the whole afternoon, and he had been given no plausible excuse for displaying his inside knowledge.

He walked about with wrinkled brows and lowered eyes as if pondering some difficult problem. But his mind was entirely devoted to that one disappointing fact. Once or twice he stopped near the places occupied by the others and regarded them disapprovingly. The ladies escaped comparatively easily. They were a lot of middle-aged spinsters, and they had already flattered him a little too much. But Engelhardt might have had a question or two to ask. What was the use of reading about crimes when real ones were being committed right under one's nose . . . and especially when one was living in the same house with one of their principal victims. And he had, for that matter, not asked about a single thing during the whole week. But it really did not make any difference. He was nothing but a soft-brained, punning moron. The case of Rognaas was far more provoking. He was a real man, and he had proved quite nice on the few occasions when he stayed at home. But he had asked no questions either. In fact, it had looked as if he didn't even care to listen.

Lydersen stood looking at him for a long time, feeling more and more irritated by his long, lean fingers that were running races with one another across the keys.

"Why does he care to do it?" Lydersen thought. "How can a grown-up person sit like that, clinking for hours on that kind of instrument? And today he is playing more nervously than he usually does."

But Rognaas must also have become irritated at Lydersen, for he broke off abruptly in the midst of a run and asked in a somewhat excited tone:

"Will you do me a favor, Lydersen?"

Lydersen looked at him in surprise. He was struck by a confused, uncomprehending dumbness that prevented him from answering. All he could do was to stare.

"Will you please take off that bandage as soon as you don't need it any longer?"

His words attracted general attention. All present

looked up from their various intellectual preoccupations and gaped in astonishment at those two.

But through Lydersen's momentary paralysis of the mind . . . right through it . . . flashed the memory of Berger's infamous remark:

"If you two had had a little more time, Kvisthus wouldn't be lying in a coffin today, and you wouldn't be wearing that decorative bandage!"

His surprise increased, and his dumbness continued. He could do nothing but gaze in bewildered confusion at the nervous face of Rognaas.

And it was the bank teller who broke the silence again.

"You wear it as if it were an Iron Cross," he said. "But I don't think there is anything heroic in acting rashly. And I have also heard from the hospital that your wound is not so very serious. It drives me crazy to have to watch that memento of heroism and suffering. I believe you might just as well take it off. I shall be glad to help you, if you care. We can pull the hair over the scar. That wouldn't look half so silly."

This was something unprecedented, an unbelievable novelty in the annals of the boarding-house. No one was able to utter a protest. No one had presence of mind enough to interfere until it was all over. And then it was too late.

For Lydersen turned around, abruptly, without a word, and left the room.

Rognaas stood looking after him, still excited, but without making a move.

Behind him one of the schoolmistresses raised her tall and righteous shape to its full height.

"Shame on you!" she said. "Shame on you, Herr Rognaas!"

Then he turned, and they saw that he was white as a corpse from nervous agitation.

"I could never have expected such a thing from you," the woman went on. "And one thing I must tell you. A man who is stricken down at his post as Lydersen was—he *is* a hero."

Rognaas threw back his head impatiently.

"Or a stupid ass!" he said.

"You ought to be ashamed of yourself . . . that's what all of us think." She turned to the others: "Am I right? And you, Herr Engelhardt, why don't you say something . . . you who are a man . . . ?"

Engelhardt put the book down, grew red in the face, and began to hem and haw.

"Of course," he said. "Yes, of course."

But the words seem to stick in his throat, and it

was all he said. Then Frøken Larsen took it upon herself to administer punishment.

"Think of Berger instead," she said. "Think of a man who could act in such unmanly fashion, who could show such absolute lack of any sense of duty. Don't you think it would be better to attack him instead?"

But Rognaas gave her a scornful glance.

"He was the only sensible one among them. He was wise. And besides, he has never annoyed me by any display of heroic bandages."

With that he turned and left them. And neither he nor Lydersen appeared again that night.

LYDERSEN did not remove the bandage until Monday morning, when he was ready to go in for breakfast. He tried to take it off that same Sunday night. But it was beyond him. When he appeared at the table next morning, looking like an ordinary human being, he suffered an impoverished sense of being past the days of his greatness.

He had been lying awake the night before, thinking of that scene in the living-room. But he could not understand it . . . found it utterly beyond his comprehension. And it was equally impossible for him to grasp how Rognaas could mean what he had said or how he could make himself say such a thing.

The lady who owned the handicrafts shop was the only other guest at the table.

She told him about the castigation of the offender and assured him that all of them had felt very indignant about it.

"Herr Engelhardt, too," she said. "I must tell you . . . he was so wrought up that he couldn't speak a word . . . and you know how fluent he is as a rule."

Shortly afterward, Herr Engelhardt appeared, and, as bad luck would have it, his attitude belied her words. Smilingly he surveyed Lydersen's head, now in mufti, so to speak. Then he raised his eyebrows in a jocular effort to register surprise. Ugly before, that grimace made him still uglier.

"Congratulations," he said, bowing slightly.

Then he sat down and began to talk of other things.

One by one, the others came in later. But Rognaas did not appear. It was in everybody's mind, but no one said a word about it. That was meant to spare Lydersen. But the ladies at least felt satisfied to have things as they were.

But when Lydersen went back to his room to get his hat and coat, Rognaas sat there waiting for him.

He looked evidently embarrassed and very nervous as he held out his hand.

"I did not mean to offend you," he said.

Lydersen accepted the proffered hand before he had time to consider whether he should do so or not. Having done that, he also became embarrassed and looked away.

"No, of course not," he said.

"It was nothing but nervousness. The reason was, I think, that it always upsets me to hear any one talk of sickness and wounds. Some people are like that. They cannot bear to think of death and annihilation. You can understand that, I hope?"

"Yes, of course."

It was not much of a consolation, but Lydersen grabbed at it, even though he was a little angry with himself for doing so. And on his way to the office, lacking the bandage, he arrived at this conclusion:

"It has given me a certain position nevertheless, and no one of my age in the service will find it easy to get by me."

III

THE HERO AND THE VICTIMS

1

THE mystery of this crass and brutal crime remained unsolved. Those that committed it seemed to have vanished from the earth. Even the finger-print experts were stumped. They found partly preserved prints on the boxes and the keys, but the clearest of these could all be traced to the office personnel. The rest were mere smears that could not be identified by comparison with the police records.

The vague suspicions that had been directed toward Berger died a natural death. There was no proof whatever involving him. And the very foundation of those suspicions was weak. During his twenty years of service he had shown more than usual devotion to his duties. Nothing but his behavior during the hold-up could have suggested him as a possible accomplice.

There was nothing to do. The case had to be dropped.

But there were two persons who never dropped it. They were Berger and Lydersen.

Neither one showed it to the other during their daily life in the office. Their colleagues never dreamt of it. But both of them were equally well aware of it. They kept an eye on each other as if to make sure how much of that incident remained alive with the other man. Externally nothing happened. They did nothing directly. But either one of them was pretty well posted in regard to the other one.

One result of this situation was that they had as little as possible to do with each other. Berger avoided Lydersen, and Lydersen let him do so, feeling that he was no longer worth bothering about.

Naturally enough, the incident had left deeper marks on Berger. To Lydersen it was always something that tickled his vanity. To Berger, on the other hand, it was a spot on his honor, a source of humiliation, that must leave any self-respecting man in a state of unhappiness. He lived in a ferment of constant, although silent, opposition to the attitude which the others had seen fit to assume. But among all the rest, Lydersen was the special enemy. He was the personification, the supreme embodiment of that attitude.

Thanks to his simple, peaceful, almost boyish nature, Berger had no tendency to develop into the kind of man who is always looking for a quarrel. On the contrary, he tried as far as possible to imagine that most people would take his side if he placed the problem directly before them. To be sure, he had neither the chance nor the courage to carry out any inquiry along those lines. But little by little he received a certain impression, although a very vague one, from the people with whom he came in contact. And to his bitter surprise it appeared that he stood practically alone.

"There are only two parties," he concluded at last. "On one side there are a little boy and myself. All other people are on the other side, with that hero, Lydersen, at their head."

One plain, ordinary man and a little boy of five arrayed against the rest of humanity . . . this represents an inferiority of strength too great to be borne. To the boy it seemed natural that his father should prefer to keep alive, no matter what he might do for that purpose. He gave no further thought to such a self-evident thing. He simply forgot all about it.

Berger, on the other hand, could never forget it. And it became an urgent matter with him to discover one or two persons who agreed with him. Unfortunately he was not acquainted with Rognaas, the bank teller. But Lydersen was. And he had no reason for making Berger aware that Rognaas existed. To him it was a particularly provoking circumstance that, apart from his peculiar opinion in this case, Rognaas was a thoroughly attractive personality.

It never occurred to Berger to scream out his discontent and his embittered rebelliousness before other people. And he never dreamt of taking them to task. Instead he was filled with pity for such a limitless and incurable stupidity. But with all his soul he hated the humiliation he had had to suffer on account of their idiotic blindness. Those days of degradation had put their stamp on him, and he was hopelessly ignorant of any means by which he could wash off the disgrace that clung to him.

It was this that roused him most . . . the fact that he found himself looked down upon . . . the fact that he had been taken for a criminal.

When first he was seized by that sense of helpless impotence—after the situation had become clear to him—he thought:

"There must be some one who understands me. Every one cannot be so stubbornly unreasonable."

He found relief in the thought that he might visit his mother to see how *she* took it. And this intention he put into effect soon after the funeral of Kvisthus.

OLD Fru Berger had been a widow for more than twenty years. She had a son and a daughter, but as both of them were married, she lived by herself. The long, lonely years, and the constant need of economy, had developed in her a spirit of quiet, reserved seriousness. She had just completed her sixtieth year, but was still slender and rather short of stature.

The night when Berger appeared, she had been reading. She carried her eyeglasses in her hand when she opened the door for him. It was already nine o'clock, and the expression on her face was one of surprise and some anxiety until she saw who it was. Then she smiled faintly and a little wearily. Perhaps that smile of hers was even a little more weary than usual.

He looked searchingly at her for a second.

"Good evening, Mother. I haven't been to see you for quite some time."

"Never mind, dear."

She spoke as if it were quite natural that she shouldn't see him oftener. And she stood waiting for him until he had taken off his coat. Then she led him into her living-room.

"Sit down."

"Thanks, Mother."

But he remained standing for a moment, and he felt, as he had sometimes done before, how much harder it was for them to establish contact with each other after he had married and had a child of his own. It made him uncertain . . . a little fearful of hurting her by not appearing affectionate enough. He had had this feeling more than once. Practically every time he left her, it was as if both of them, without meaning to do so, had wasted a warmth which they could not transmit to each other.

When he was seated, he looked over at her . . . with the air of a little boy, but with the same uncertainty as before.

"How are you feeling, Mother?"

She was still standing, and he could see an expression of fatigue pass across her face. But it disappeared instantaneously.

"Thank you," she said. "I am quite well, fortunately."

A pause followed. Berger did not know what to say, and when his mother also remained silent, he grabbed at the only thing he could think of.

"Have you heard from Inga recently?"

"Yes, I had a letter from her last Saturday."

"And everything is all right?"

"Yes, all four of them are doing well. Would you care to read her letter?"

"Thanks . . . yes."

He embraced the chance eagerly, and he began to whistle softly while his mother looked for the letter. When she brought it, he rose to receive it. And he remained standing while he opened it a little slowly. Then he put the envelope on the table and took another chair while reading the letter. It looked as if he felt it necessary to keep moving, lest they suddenly should be sitting there without anything to say or do.

Fortunately enough, the letter was written the very day when the hold-up occurred. Consequently it could not contain any references to that event. The tone was sweet and friendly, and she sent her regards to him. All this served to reassure him.

"They are doing well," he said. "Don't you think so?"

His mother nodded.

"Yes," she said, "*they* are doing well."

The barely noticeable emphasis she put on the word "they" was enough to attract his attention. He gave her a furtive glance while he was folding up the letter. But she had picked up her book from the table and was now putting it back on the shelf. He waited until this was done before he replaced the letter in the envelope and handed it back to her.

"Thanks," he said.

His mother received the letter in silence. Then she asked:

"Have you had supper?"

"Yes, thank you."

"Is there nothing I can offer you? I have some fruit . . ."

There was eagerness behind his refusal.

"No, thank you. Let us sit down for a talk instead. Have you nothing new to tell me?"

His mother sat down, and his nervous anxiety made him think that there was a questioning look in her calm and wise eyes. But all she said was:

"No, I don't think so. Nothing ever happens where I am."

Then he picked up courage to approach the difficult point.

"No," he said with an attempt at levity, "a whole lot more happens elsewhere."

They looked at each other. Then both of them looked away again. And there was a brief pause.

Then his mother asked:

"How are you feeling?"

"Thank you," he replied. "You know . . . ?"

He gave her a scrutinizing glance. She nodded as her eyes met his.

"Yes, I do," she said.

It seemed to him that an expression of disappointment crept into her face. Then he could hold out no longer. He must know where he had her.

"Mother," he asked, "are you disappointed in me?"

His question sounded as if it had been asked by a scared boy. She took time to answer, and her answer was evasive.

"No," she said, "not disappointed . . ."

"Do you think that I acted wrongly?"

She looked at him calmly but with a suggestion of wonder in her glance.

"I suppose you did what *you* thought was right?"

He was carried away by a sudden craving to break down her reserve.

"Yes, I did, Mother. But other people don't seem to think that it was the right thing. They simply believe that I was frightened. But that was not the case. I merely thought that it wasn't worth the price of my life."

His mother's face softened a little.

"Was that what you thought?"

"Yes, Mother. I did not see why I should die for such a sum. But perhaps you think differently?"

She gave him an incredulous glance.

"Die? Do you really believe he would have shot you?"

"Yes," he replied firmly. "That's the way he looked. And then I didn't think . . . but perhaps you do?"

There was a suggestion of helplessness in his question, and it made the mother feel helpless too.

"Oh," she said, "what I think . . . I am nothing but an old woman. I don't know anything about such things."

"But you have heard other people talk?"

Once more his mother's face took on that tired look. But it also carried a suggestion of pain.

"Yes, I have," she admitted. "But they say so much. You know how people are."

Beyond that point they could not get. They felt depressed and perplexed. Now and then they looked at each other, and Berger was drumming nervously on the table. As soon as he noticed what he was doing, he stopped and pushed his hand through his hair. A moment later he rose, his mind made up.

"I must go," he said. "You want to go to bed soon."

"Not at all," she said. "As far as I am concerned, my boy, you may just as well stay."

Berger was touched by the tenderness of her tone. He took her by the shoulders, held her in front of himself, and looked hard at her.

"I fear you are disappointed in me after all?"

But she stuck it out bravely.

"Not at all," she assured him.

"Is that really the truth, Mother?"

"Yes, indeed."

Then he seemed to understand just how she felt, and with a sick feeling in his heart he went out into the hall to put on his coat. She followed him.

"Come back soon," she begged him. "As soon as you can find time."

"I shall, Mother. Good-night!"

"Good-night . . . and remember me at home."

"Thanks."

He had to pass a dark courtyard and a narrow passage before he reached the street. There he stopped a moment as if uncertain as to what he should do next. Then he shrugged his shoulders and walked away in a mood of embittered resignation.

"Yes," he said to himself, trying desperately to make light of it, "that was that!"

But as he walked, his burden grew more and more heavy. That sense of frustrated resentment took hold of him again. It was not directed against his mother, but against everything and everybody. One moment it occurred to him that he might have a talk with Lydersen. In the next he realized the futility of such a step.

"No," he thought, "all I can do is to swallow it and keep silent... no matter how much it hurts. But what you hide is not necessarily forgotten. And it is strange anyhow that I am alive. I really ought to be dead. Strictly speaking, I have no right to be walking here."

Then it began to drizzle, and he hastened his steps. Preoccupied as he was, he did not notice another pedestrian until he walked right into him and nearly knocked him down. He muttered some excuses and was about to walk on, when he observed that the other man had stopped, looking as if he wanted something.

"Pardon me," he said, "but can you tell me what time it is?"

Berger looked mechanically at his watch.

"About ten," he replied.

"So late as that? And now it's beginning to rain

again. There must be an awful lot of rain in this city."

Something in the man's tone aroused Berger's attention.

"Yes," he agreed. "You don't belong here, do you?"

"No, I have lived here only a short time. I don't know the place very well yet. I don't think we have ever met before."

Berger looked at the man in surprise and shook his head.

"No," he said, "not as far as I can remember."

The other one put a couple of fingers to the brim of his hat in salute.

"Well, many thanks. I guess this side street is mine."

Berger remained standing at the corner, looking after him.

"That was almost like old times," he thought, "when I could talk with somebody without being afraid of what might be said."

2

BERGER, for that matter, was not the only one who suffered from what had happened. Fru Kvisthus had her share of it, too. Perhaps her suffering was not as acute as that of Berger, but it was probably more painful in one way. In spite of everything, Berger nourished a dim hope, a sort of fatalistic conviction, buried deeply in his subconscious mind, that one day he would be exonerated . . . that one day some new development, whether miraculous or natural, would place everything in a different light. He had no idea of how this might happen, or what lines it might take. He merely *willed* that such a thing should happen.

Fru Kvisthus, on the other hand, had nothing at all to hope for. Her husband *was* dead. And no one who stands beside a newly made grave can bear in mind the possibility that passing years and new habits may still the sorrow and wipe out all regrets.

He *was* dead. He had gone elsewhere . . . if he had gone anywhere at all. Sometimes she doubted it, and at other times she seemed to sense his physical and spiritual proximity. But to ask for him was of no use . . . not of the least use any longer.

A couple of days passed before she fully realized the dreadful fact that everything had come to an irrevocable end. During the first hours of feverish panic, she simply refused to accept that fact. Not until the coffin had been taken to the chapel did she quite grasp that she was left alone with her son. Then her eyes were opened, and she saw what actually had happened: They had killed Kvisthus, and now he was lying in a white coffin, in a cold and dark stone vault, waiting to be buried for ever. That was how reality looked to her.

But it is one thing to see and recognize reality, and quite another to accept its yoke in a spirit of submission . . . to become reconciled to it, such as it is.

This was what Fru Kvisthus could not do. She rose in open rebellion. She bombarded heaven with desperately challenging questions.

"Why should this happen to him? Why might it not just as well have happened to one of the other two? Was there any reason why three humble and contented people like ourselves should not be permitted to go on living and being happy together? In what manner had we sinned so that we must be punished?"

After the funeral she stayed at home day and night. Her parents and relatives visited her, but she rejected their consolations in a spirit of dumb helplessness . . . like a child that cannot understand and is unwilling to submit to what it does not understand. They all left her with a sense of having been unable to help her. And so she was left alone with her son. But a child is a child, and the end of it was that she found herself completely alone . . . deserted and hopeless.

No ONE thought more frequently of her during those days than did Berger. Subsequent to the "reconciliation" that took place between himself and Helen after the Kvisthus funeral, there followed a time when Helen took back the hand she had held out to him. The hardness of those first and most bitter days had left her, to be sure, but many trifling occurrences showed him that she still carried a sense of humiliation in her heart.

"But for a reason that is the very opposite of hers," Berger thought, "Esther carries in her heart a much more serious wound. Perhaps it would do them both good to meet again and talk it over."

One afternoon, when he was free from the office, he made the suggestion to Helen.

"I don't think you have visited her since the day it happened."

But she refused in a peculiar spirit of suppressed bitterness.

"Later on," she said. "But not just now."

He looked at her in surprise.

"Will it be easier later on?"

To this she gave no answer at all. Instead she withdrew into herself, behind a wall of prohibitive defiance. It made him shake his head with a sense of frustration.

"For heaven's sake," he said, "*she* can't help it, can she? And we have been close enough to make it seem unreasonable for us to keep away from her when she is in trouble."

Her face grew hard and impatient while he talked.

"Don't torment me," she said. "If one of us must go, you had better go yourself."

He understood that she meant this to settle the question, and he bowed his head in disappointment and shame. At the same time, however, anger aroused in him a spirit of contrariness that made him suddenly rise.

"All right," he said, "I'll do that."

Without paying any attention to her incredulous and surprised glance, he went out and put on his coat. In his innermost soul he expected and hoped that she would offer to take his place, or that, at least, she would persuade him to stay at home. He knew that the latter alternative was in her mind. But she hardened herself and did not move. And he left.

Down the stairs, and for a while in the street, he walked slowly. Then he was seized by a hope and a thought that made the visit seem more desirable.

"Who knows," he thought, "whether something good may not come of it?"

ESTHER KVISTHUS gave him an indifferent and unrecognizing glance as she opened the door. Then an expression of surprise appeared on her face.

"Erik!" she cried. "Are *you* coming to see *me?*"

The astonishment and the ache with which those words were fraught made him feel confused at first. His own suffering turned suddenly into a mere nothing, and hers became everything.

"Yes, I am coming to see you," he said, "and to find out how you are feeling. To be of any real help is out of the question, I fear."

Then she gave him a prolonged look and a note of appeal came into her voice.

"Who knows, Erik?" she said. "Who knows?"

He followed her in a state of bewilderment that depressed him deeply. And all the time he seemed to hear those plaintive and strangely pleading words: "Who knows, Erik? Who knows?" It sounded as if she placed some kind of hope in him, and he was ashamed of realizing that he had come not only to give, but to receive.

"Sit down," she urged. "It seems so strange to find you here, of all people."

An atmosphere of restlessness surrounded her. When she had mastered her feelings to some extent, she said resentfully:

"It is so dreadful to think that we have a home here, and that he will never see it again. He prized everything in this place because it belonged to us. And now it will be scattered. I cannot keep all of it. What's the use of my keeping it? Next to his death, this thought is what troubles me most."

Then he asked cautiously:

"Why don't you try to keep it?"

She shook her head.

"No," she said, "it can't be done. How far do you think my small pension will go? Oh, no . . . we shall have to move into a smaller and cheaper place. You must remember that I have the boy. And we were so anxious to give him a good start."

She made a sudden movement as if about to burst into tears, and she had to keep silent in order to control herself. Suffering and bitterness showed in the contraction of her lips.

"That thousand kroner," she said. "I shall try to save with that in mind."

Berger had to look away. He felt drenched with shame, as if he himself had been a party to the assessment of the dead man's value.

A little later she said:

"I am not complaining. I suppose it couldn't be otherwise. But it is hard to think that the boy and I must suffer poverty on top of everything else. I understand we shall be granted a larger pension than is the rule. But we shall have less to live on nevertheless."

Berger rose.

"Yes," he said indignantly, "the least thing they could have done was to see that you and the boy were freed from economic cares. Your other loss should have been enough in itself."

She stood looking at him, a new hardness appearing in her eyes . . . as if once more there was something she had difficulty in controlling.

"Yes," she said, "that was the main one . . . his death. The minister said that he would learn . . . why it had to happen. And I suppose he meant that I also should learn that much some time. But until I do, Erik . . . until I do . . . ?"

Berger shook his head, knowing that he could do nothing.

"Yes, yes," was all he could say.

Her glance, at once timid and hard, evaded his.

"I have discovered something lately," she said. "It is easy to console, but difficult to become consoled."

Berger looked down.

"Yes," he said. "My position has not been an easy one either."

"No. I know it. But you are alive, after all."

He shrugged his shoulders.

"Yes . . . but who cares about that . . . except myself."

She raised her face protestingly.

"Oh!" she said, "Helen and Leif . . ."

"Yes . . . Leif."

His tone was so pitiful that it startled himself. She looked at him as if she couldn't believe her own ears.

"But Helen?"

Without looking up, he answered evasively:

"Yes, she did care . . . that first evening. But now they have spoiled everything for her."

Esther Kvisthus shook her head.

"You are mistaken, Erik. I know that Arne died . . . like a hero, I think they call it. In a way I am proud that he did what he should do. But I should much prefer that he had been scared."

Berger gave a start and looked up apprehensively. "Scared?" he repeated.

But she was not listening. She was entirely lost in consideration of that other possibility.

Then he left her, deeply disturbed. And he heard her say behind him . . . not to him, but to herself . . . or to no one in particular:

"I really didn't want to blame him."

3

HIS visit to Fru Kvistus left a sting behind. In a state of puzzled dejection he recalled the scene in the cemetery and the words she had spoken on that occasion. Out of her own distress she had then offered him the understanding which all others denied him. And of all the people in the world, who was in a better position than she to understand?

"But now," he thought, "now she is making reservations. With all her soul she wishes that he might still be alive. But at the same time she does not like to miss the halo of heroism which they have bestowed on him. Oh, Kvisthus . . . poor Kvisthus!"

No, it was more than he could understand. Just as he couldn't understand Helen. But he felt no pronounced bitterness against her either.

"It will pass, by and by," he reassured himself. "All she needs is time. At bottom she feels just as I do about it. It is only the other people who have made her feel differently."

And he thought of "the other people" with genuine bitterness, in a spirit of painful, irreconcilable hostility . . . all those who had been ready to condemn him. In the front rank of these he placed the postmaster and Commissioner Lier, both of whom had attacked him directly. Back of these he placed all those who had not had the courage to say anything openly. And back of these again the whole unknown horde that had talked and talked.

But ahead of all the rest, he placed Lydersen. He was most closely involved. He was the proved enemy.

"Yes," he thought, "if any concession were made to me, that man would feel it a violation of his own rights. But we'll see. He is not dead yet. Perhaps a time will come when he will take a different view of it."

There was no threat in that final thought. It merely expressed an obstinate hope.

THAT ARMED truce between Berger and Lydersen lasted a whole year. Then occurred something that brought about what resembled an open collision.

One of the division chiefs in the office was transferred to another city, and he left a vacancy behind. Berger had reached the age when he could hope to get the appointment, but of this he said nothing to Helen.

Then she asked him one day at the table:

"Isn't Herr Ruud going to move?"

"Yes," Berger assented, blushing slightly. "How do you happen to know?"

"Others have told me."

A little later she asked:

"Do you mean to apply for the position?"

He gave her an astonished look.

"Well . . . I have thought of it at least."

She hesitated a moment before she summoned up the courage to ask one more question:

"Have you any hope of getting it?"

He laughed . . . a forced and harsh laughter.

"Yes, of course . . . unless they give preference to Lydersen."

He saw her lose color.

"But you are the older one," she said with determination.

He shrugged his shoulders.

"Yes . . . but he has more courage."

Their eyes avoided each other. Nearly a year had passed since they referred to that incident.

Nothing more was said between them about his application or his chances of promotion. But Berger did file an application, and when the time for doing so was up, he was the oldest man on the list. Lydersen was number four. Both spent the ensuing period in a state of tense expectation. For one man it was a question of holding his own advantage, while the object of the other one was to push ahead of him. For a month they did not look at each other . . . not even when their work forced them to speak to each other. It was like a silent and hateful duel which, after all, could not be decided by themselves.

Both thought:

"If I don't get it, I hope at least that he doesn't, but that the place goes to one of those two between us."

Their colleagues also discussed the situation, but their eagerness was checked by certain scruples. They grew silent when one of those two approached. Although most of them hoped that Berger would get it, they thought Lydersen had the better chance.

The egoism of Lydersen suffered severely.

"I must get by him," he thought. "It's my right . . . after what happened that time."

On the other hand, it was the self-respect of Berger that was at stake.

"If he should lose," he thought, "he has in reality lost nothing. He has simply failed to win. But if I lose, it will be a real loss. It will mean the loss of everything."

At home both he and Helen were stirred by an anxiety which they did not care to admit to each other. During those critical days, Berger was met by a questioning, frightened look whenever he came through the door. It was a look that anticipated disaster, but that clung to hope nevertheless and that pleaded for information as quickly as possible.

It was Lydersen who got it. The notification came early one morning, when both were on duty. It was sent in from the sorting-room by a loud-voiced special-delivery messenger, who proclaimed the news on his way in, fully aware of the sensation he was causing.

Berger was alone in his room, busy with his accounts. But the door was open, and he could not help hearing.

For a moment he was seized by an attack of vertigo. He could feel that his face turned white, and his hand shook so that he had to drop the pen. Far in, within the innermost recesses of his being, there was something that gnawed and gnawed . . . a horrible mixture of sorrow, humiliation, disappointment, and hatred.

He let out a subdued groan and found it a relief to be alone.

But suddenly he slapped the book in front of him with the palm of his hand. And a thought flashed through him, wild and desperate, full of dire distress:

"What are you whining about? You knew it all the time. Why in hell did you file an application? You knew in advance what would happen!"

But at the same moment he knew also that he had to make that application, no matter how sure he was of his own defeat . . . that, in fact, he had made it to be confirmed in his certainty.

And now . . . now he had what he had looked for. The certainty he had felt was now confirmed.

By a violent effort he pulled himself together and picked up the pen again. But he found it difficult to resume his writing. He had to do it very slowly and carefully, and yet he could see that what he wrote was nothing but a caricature of his regular hand.

When his task was finished, he rose and went in to Lydersen. The victor looked up, but there was more of embarrassment and fear than triumph in his glance. For the first time in many months their eyes met fully.

"Congratulations."

"Thanks."

Lydersen tried awkwardly to rise, but Berger had already turned about and was on his way back to his own room. His legs did not obey him very well, and he had a feeling of being stared at by the rest after he had passed. At any rate that return of his was accompanied by a peculiar stillness.

At nine o'clock he went in to the postmaster.

"I should like to have an application blank."

His voice was toneless, and the glance he received was uneasy.

"Why? What are you applying for?"

Berger did not reply. He merely waited, rigid and immovable. His hand was still trembling when he received the blank. Without a word he went back to his desk and wrote out an application for a position at the post-office in the capital. Then he returned to the postmaster's office and handed it over in silence.

He pretended not to see the surprise with which it was received. He merely saluted and went out.

All this he did without giving any clear thought to what he was doing. He merely felt that it was the only proper and natural thing to do . . . that he had planned it long ago in some part of his subconscious mind.

Twice during the morning Lydersen passed by his desk. Each time he seemed to lag, as if he were thinking of stopping. But each time he passed on.

Berger observed him uneasily.

"I guess," he thought, "that he has found out. And so have the others, I suppose."

A hard bitterness filled his mind.

"He looked as if he meant to condole with me."

Two o'clock came, and both went off duty. When Berger entered the cloak-room, Lydersen was already there with his coat on. He was busy making up a parcel, and it seemed to take him a long time to get it done. Only when Berger had washed and was drying his hands did Lydersen turn to leave. He placed the parcel under his arm, as if hesitating about something. And suddenly their eyes met. They really looked at each other.

Something had to happen. They could not part like that.

Lydersen hemmed a little. The situation caused him to look pale and somewhat solemn.

"I hear that you are applying for a transfer," he said.

Berger went on wiping his hands.

"Yes," he replied curtly.

"I hope that you are not doing it on my account?"

"What do you mean by that?"

Lydersen's sense of uncertainty made him awkwardly patronizing.

"You don't have to be afraid of me," he said.

"Afraid?"

"Yes . . . I have no intention of treating you unfairly."

Berger dropped the towel and stared at the man. Then he burst suddenly into laughter.

It was a harsh and scornful laugh that puzzled Lydersen.

"What are you laughing at?" he asked with an offended mien.

Berger laughed still more loudly and with intense abandon.

Then Lydersen straightened himself up, full of dignified resentment.

"You don't need to act like an idiot," he said.

And when Berger went right on laughing, he turned and closed the door behind him with a violent bang.

BERGER himself did not know what had made him laugh. "Unless it was to keep myself from crying like a woman," he thought, as he walked home in a perplexed and discouraged state of mind. But that laughter had let something loose within himself and he felt weakened by it. He dreaded to get home and have to give an account of himself.

As soon as he entered the door, he was met by the same apprehensive inquiry. Generally he responded with a shake of his head. Today he pretended not to see. But silence also constitutes a reply, and he could see that there was no question left to answer. It made him still more nervous.

"That was your chance," he thought. "It will be much harder to speak later."

And his own evasiveness also gave him a pang of bad conscience in regard to Helen. This, too, tended to increase his nervousness, but he tried hard to hide it.

Not until they were drinking their coffee did he say:

"While I think of it . . . I have to congratulate you on account of Lydersen."

Both of them blushed deeply.

"So it did go . . . to him?"

Her voice was barely audible.

He nodded brusquely.

"It did," he said.

Helen gazed at him until her eyes grew dim with tears. She did not really weep. The tears merely welled out. But the fact that she sat still, saying nothing, made it much worse for him.

"Why don't you say something?" he asked pleadingly.

But she only shook her head.

A moment later she rose and left the table. Her cup of coffee was only half emptied. He heard her go into the bedroom and sit down there. He himself remained sitting where he was in the dusk, feeling vacuous and finished.

After a while she returned. She was then over the worst. Having thrown out the cold coffee, she poured herself a fresh cup.

He could see that her hand was still trembling a little. And it hurt him. Suddenly it burst out of him like a sigh through the darkness:

"I wish it might be cleared up some time."

She turned her eyes slowly toward him, looking at him almost as if he were a stranger. But she understood what he meant. And she noticed that his thin face wore a peculiarly poverty-stricken expression.

"Do you think it would help?"

She was sitting with her chin resting in one of her hands, staring straight ahead of her.

"Yes," he said. "Then they would understand that I had no other chance . . . that my life really was at stake."

A sense of restlessness seized him. He rose and began to walk about.

A while later she asked from behind his back:

"What are you going to do now?"

"I have applied for a transfer," he answered.

Then he turned around to watch the effect of that news on her.

She let out a sigh of relief.

"Thank heaven!"

After another pause, she asked:

"To where?"

"To Oslo . . . there is more seclusion in a large city."

He had resumed his walking . . . timid and distracted.

Then she spoke again from behind his back, but in a harder tone than before.

"You should not have done that!"

He turned, now on his guard.

"What should I not have done?"

Without raising her face, she said in a voice that quivered with excitement:

"What you did that time. You might have shown a *little* more courage."

He looked at her without replying. His glance showed that he was profoundly stirred. She looked up and noticed it.

"Yes," she said defiantly, "I mean it. We shall have to pay for it as long as we live. This is what you get for that."

"And what of it?" he asked in an agitated tone.

"What of it?"

He came a step closer to her.

"You forget that I am alive," he said, "even though every one begrudges me the fact."

When she stared at him without answering, he went up quite close to her and repeated with passionate intensity:

"I am *alive* . . . I am *alive* . . . I am *alive!*"

Then he turned about and walked away from her. She sat still, with a colorless face, shaken to the very depths of her being.

4

THE evening paper carried a notice of Lydersen's promotion. It forced him to celebrate at the boarding-house, with madeira for the ladies and high-balls for the men. Lydersen was close in money matters, although not exactly stingy. He surrendered unwillingly to the inevitable, and only after many broad hints, but when he had taken the plunge, he provided plenty of good wine and whiskey really worth drinking. When the fun began, he put the bottles on the table with a lot of self-satisfied pride in the brands displayed.

They gathered in the living-room after supper, and their number was complete, not to say replete, as Herr Engelhardt put it.

Lydersen was a slightly embarrassed but rather engaging host, displaying a certain indolent sociability. It was not easy for him to put aside the reserved and surly dignity that served as his everyday front. To appear as the center of a triumph gave him a faintly intoxicating sense of importance, but on the other hand he was not accustomed to act as host, and the duties of doing so weighed heavily on him.

But Frøken Larsen, the teacher who acted as spokesman for the ladies, gave him stout assistance and support. Not only did she take charge of the practical arrangements, but she also delivered what might be called the address of the occasion.

It came after they had drunk the first, rather lukewarm, and somewhat forced toast of congratulation.

"That's what it means to be a hero," she said. "And it is pleasant to see virtue rewarded at times. For I understand that you were not at all the oldest applicant, Herr Lydersen."

"No, three of them were older than I," he said. Then he looked around cautiously before he went on: "Berger was the oldest . . . and he is two years older than I."

"The man who gave up the money?"

"Yes."

Frøken Larsen nodded her silent but conclusive appreciation.

But one of the engineers rubbed his nose pensively with his left forefinger as he looked up and spoke loudly into the silence that had ensued:

"But that's a devilish procedure nevertheless."

His words had an instantaneously depressing effect . . . or at least they served to subdue their enthusiasm. They looked from one to another. The whole affair seemed near a collapse, and the offender looked guiltily nonplussed. But, to the relief of Lydersen, the situation was saved by Frøken Larsen.

Until then he had suffered a faint but astonishing pang of bad conscience.

"Pardon me, Herr Iversen," she said, "but what exactly do you mean?"

Iversen scratched his neck in momentary confusion.

"What I meant?" he repeated. "I was thinking of that other poor devil."

"Well, what about him? You were thinking of Berger?"

Iversen squirmed under the need of getting out of it.

"Of course," he said, "I didn't mean to defend that fellow. It merely struck me that it must feel like the devil . . . I beg your pardon! . . . to be left behind like an idiot."

"Would you have given up the money?"

"Of course not. That was a silly thing to do."

Frøken Larsen surveyed him sternly, with the authority of a disciplinarian.

"Well, then . . . what more need be said?"

There was no help for it. Iversen had been put in the dunce's corner. And with self-satisfied pride Frøken Larsen pushed some thin, grayish-yellow curls away from her forehead.

Lydersen hadn't enjoyed it at all. Several times

he glared disapprovingly at Herr Iversen. And with a certain Sunday evening and a certain Monday morning still fresh in his memory, he also kept a watchful eye on Rognaas and Engelhardt. Rognaas had looked interested and in accord with the opinion expressed . . . that is, the one at first expressed by Iversen. But Engelhardt had appeared merely interested, and his interest was devoted to Frøken Larsen.

"How did he take it?" Rognaas asked.

Lydersen was somewhat slow in answering.

"He laughed rather hysterically."

After a pause, he felt that he must say more than that, as, after all, he was the center of the affair. Looking around at those present, he remarked defensively:

"*I* can't help it, as far as I can see."

Then Engelhardt burst into laughter.

"You don't look it, Lydersen, but you are a sly one. I can see that you are fishing. But there is no need of it as long as Frøken Larsen is here."

Lydersen gave him a wrathful look. After that he didn't know what to do with his eyes. And he sat staring at the table until some kindly soul proposed another drink.

The face of Frøken Larsen also grew more stern. When they had had the drink, she looked reprovingly at Engelhardt before she turned solemnly to Lydersen and said:

"It's quite true that Herr Lydersen does not need to go fishing. We are all agreed that he acted like a man. And it is not his fault if the other one is left behind . . . 'like an idiot.' The Bible is quite right when it says: Let the dead bury the dead!"

Lydersen was so embarrassed that he didn't know whether or not to acknowledge those remarks. To be on the safe side, he changed his position on the chair and cleared his throat.

Then Rognaas spoke up, his voice clear and penetrating, although it quivered slightly under the intensity of his conviction:

"But that is just the trouble . . . that the dead man is *not* dead!"

Frøken Larsen bristled.

"Now . . . really!"

But Rognaas went on obstinately.

"Yes," he said, "it is clear that he should have resisted, so that by this time he would have been duly buried."

Frøken Larsen gave him a supercilious look.

"You don't know *anything* about it!"

But he would not be put in the dunce's corner. He looked back at her, red in the face.

"Do you?"

"No," she admitted, "I don't, of course. But I have probability on my side."

"If you'll pardon me . . . suppose it should be on my side."

"What do you mean?"

"I mean that there is no probability involved at all. We have to deal only with a possibility . . . the possibility of being shot. And it was to that possibility he gave proper consideration."

Frøken Larsen shook her head sadly. To show her contempt for such a view, she left the retort to be delivered by the lady owner of the handicrafts shop, who sat beside her. A sarcastic smile was playing around the thin lips of this lady.

"I didn't think," she said, "that in the hour of danger any man would stop to consider the risk. But Berger was scared, of course."

Rognaas slammed down his glass on the table.

"That's pure rot," he said. "And suppose he was scared . . . what of it?"

Disconcerted and suddenly rendered a little uncertain of her position, she gave him a glance that nevertheless asserted her own superiority.

"Well, what of it?"

Rognaas looked her straight in the eye.

"Then he had a perfect right to be scared... without being damned for ever. You see, even a man has a right to give some thought to the only life that has been granted him."

"But Lydersen, who is sitting over there?"

That was a trump card. But the one on behalf of whom it was played turned red in the face and looked at Rognaas with an expression that was more hostile than self-confident. Rognaas, on his side, shrugged his shoulders wearily and let the whole thing drop.

"Yes, Lydersen . . . ," he said. And it sounded as if he had dropped Lydersen too.

Frøken Larsen left him severely alone and turned to Engelhardt.

"And you, Herr Engelhardt," she asked, "what would you have done?"

He looked back at her, raised his glass halfway, and smiled his spare, rather unbecoming smile.

"I am afraid I should have bowed politely and said: Please help yourself. But, of course, I don't think any one else ought to do the same. I am not *that* lacking in social consciousness."

Frøken Larsen drew back as from something too disgusting.

"You talk nonsense!" she told him.

Engelhardt bowed smilingly.

"Yes," he said, "the Lord gave me the part of Uriah."

Then Lydersen raised his head from the high-ball, moodily and irascibly, and at last his pent-up wrath was given a channel of escape.

"How can *you* talk of being a Uriah?" he demanded sarcastically. "You who are not married?"

After that he looked around in confusion to discover why all the others laughed. But he couldn't make it out.

Even Frøken Larsen was laughing.

IV

A FRIENDSHIP

1

DURING the next few years Berger went about waiting for a miracle . . . the miracle that was to justify him, not with the people . . . they were too many . . . but against the one who represented all of them, namely, that hero Lydersen.

And strange to say, a miracle sometimes does occur in this intricate and complicated world. It may not appear in the form we expect. It did not appear in that form to Berger. But it occurred nevertheless. It came in a shape he had never imagined, suddenly and surprisingly, stirringly and glaringly.

First came long, monotonous years. Now and then he grew impatient and discouraged. But even in such moments of weakness he knew that the miracle must occur. The orderly arrangement of this world depended on it. Justice itself depended on it. And who was he that such great principles should come to grief through his very humble and all but forgotten fate?

In the third year his mother died. It caused him a great deal of grief, and not the least because he would never be able to go to her and say: "Do you see now, Mother, that I was right after all? Now you need not be ashamed of me any longer." But his sorrow was accompanied by a certain relief. His impatience lost its goad. Now there was no such pressing haste as before.

His days were divided between the office and his home, and he did not seem to age at all. His continued astonishment at what had happened, his anger, and his expectation of a change kept him young. These emotions combined to preserve an element of boyish uprightness that had always characterized him. His bitterness never got the better of his essential kindliness.

Once Helen asked him if he wouldn't apply again for promotion. He refused timidly, saying that it was of no use. Then she suggested that he should pay a personal visit to the heads of the service in order to ask them directly whether he was not yet regarded worthy of a better chance. This he also refused to do.

On the other hand, he applied for economy's sake to be transferred to the railway-mail department. Then they could go on living where they were, while he would get an annual allowance of one thousand kroner for expenses.

During this period he had no real friends. A certain comradeship existed between him and some of his colleagues, but he never visited their homes and he never brought any one of them to his own home. No one among them could become to him what Kvisthus had been. Furthermore, the tragic death of his friend and his own connection with it had made him fearful of any more intimate acquaintanceships. He knew that such relationships always produced a greater frankness of expression, and this frankness easily led to impertinent and tactless questions and hints.

Helen also preferred things as they were. She made a few new friends, but these had no connection with her husband's line of work, and so it was not likely that they could be familiar with that unfortunate incident of the past. Before they moved, she paid a few visits to Fru Kvisthus, but they could not recover their old happy freedom from constraint, and after the removal the two women had no communication at all with each other . . . except for a single call by Fru Kvisthus on the day after the funeral of Helen's mother-in-law.

TWO LIVING AND ONE DEAD

THEY HAD lived in Oslo seven years when Berger made a new acquaintance. It happened an evening in the fall. Helen and the boy had gone to visit her parents during three days when the schools were closed. Berger came back to the Eastern Depot after one of his trips. He was tired and hungry and made straight for a restaurant to get something to eat before going home.

The place was full, and he had to walk through the whole length of it before he found an empty table in a corner. He ordered a chop and a glass of beer, and, tired as he was, he began to eat without thinking of anything in particular. The noise and bustle around him had a quieting effect on his nerves, and as soon as he had eaten he lighted his pipe and began more or less absent-mindedly to study all those people who came and went and tarried around him.

He knew no one, but all of them seemed very close to him. The purpose that brought them there was the same as his own. Back of every one lay a day of labor, and not one among them wished him any harm.

While still in this congenial mood, he discovered a man of about the same age as himself who stood in the middle of the floor surveying the over-crowded place with an air of uncertainty. At that very moment the glance of Berger encountered that of the stranger, who seemed to be trying to make up his mind.

"I think he would like to sit down here," Berger thought, "and he is wondering whether he dares."

The situation interested him, and his glance continued to meet the stranger's, but without any direct invitation in it.

The stranger hesitated a moment longer. He was still trying to make up his mind and looked slightly embarrassed. Then he approached slowly and stopped in front of the table with an uncertain smile.

"There's an awful crowd here. May I?"

Berger gave him a friendly look.

"By all means."

"Thank you!"

The stranger bowed slightly and sat down right opposite Berger, who generously moved his own dishes in order to make more room for the newcomer.

A waitress came up and took the order of the new guest. He only wanted something to drink. When he had given his order, he looked inquiringly at Berger, who all the time had watched the man with furtive interest.

Both of them felt somewhat embarrassed, and the stranger smiled apologetically.

"I am a slave of habit," he said. "I must have a cup of strong coffee before I go to bed."

"Does it not interfere with your sleep?"

"It does, but then I am fully awake at least. It is much worse to be sitting there half asleep."

Berger glanced at the cup.

"And you don't use any cream?"

"No . . . I take no cream."

There was a pause, but both of them seemed anxious to continue their talk.

After a while the other one said:

"I have never seen you here before."

Berger smiled.

"No," he said. "I am also a slave of habit and a domestic animal. As a rule, I stay at home in the evening. But just now I happen to be a grass widower."

The other one nodded, and he also smiled.

"I come here often," he said. "But, of course, I am not married."

"And not even engaged?"

The stranger put his hand on the table.

"As you can see, I am not. And that is fortunate.

I shouldn't care to be responsible for any one but myself."

There was something in the man's tone that aroused the attention of Berger.

"Do you really mean that?" he asked.

The other one evaded the question with a smile.

"Lord," he said, "we all have our weaknesses."

Shortly afterward, he looked at his watch.

"It is close to eleven," he reported, "and I should really be going. I have to go to work in the morning again."

Berger nodded.

"I have a day off. You see, I am travelling with the railway mail, and then we have every other day free."

They remained sitting for a few minutes more. Then they paid their checks at the same time and walked out together. On the street they bade each other good-night and went their different ways.

Berger experienced a mild sense of pleasure akin to what he had felt one evening, after a visit to his mother, when he stopped in the drizzle to exchange a few casual words with a passer-by. Wistfully he recalled that earlier incident.

"I have got no farther today," he thought.

DURING the days that followed Berger thought often of the stranger and the brief hour they had spent together. He did so even after the return of Helen and the boy.

"I shouldn't object to meeting him again," he confessed to himself. "He struck me as being the right kind of fellow."

Unconsciously he compared him with Kvisthus, whom he had never been able to forget. And yet there was no resemblance between them. The one thing they seemed to have in common was that you could talk to both of them without any effort.

Now and then Berger had to smile at his own naïveté.

"I don't know him at all, and yet I act as if I knew a lot about his ways. He may prove a very different sort when you come to know him better. And he is certainly no Kvisthus. There was more jollity and friendliness in Kvisthus. But if he had lived, he might not be the same now as he used to be. We all fade a little with the passing years."

Having missed that unknown man for about a week, Berger stopped one evening at the same restaurant, choosing the same hour as before. With an embarrassed and somewhat guilty feeling, he ordered nothing but coffee, took refuge behind his pipe, and began to wait. His eyes were on the entrance all the time, expectantly, and yet he knew that he would blush like a boy if the man he was waiting for should turn up.

No one came, however, and Berger went home in a state of great disappointment. The next night he repeated the experiment with exactly the same result. Then he gave it up with a sigh of discouraged resignation, lest Helen find out what he was doing, begin to question him, and conclude that he was crazy.

NEVERTHELESS they met again exactly a fortnight after their first meeting. Once more Berger was on his way home from the depot. He was crossing Carl Johan Street opposite the fire station, when, simultaneously, they discovered each other. They greeted each other with an embarrassed smile. The stranger, who already had reached the sidewalk, stopped and waited for Berger.

"So," he said, "you have been travelling again?"

Berger had a sensation of soft, grateful warmth about his heart.

"Yes," he said in high spirits, "one day is just like the other. No, that's not right either. Every other day is just like every other day. And I suppose you are on your way to that cup of black coffee?"

The other one nodded and asked in a casual tone, without looking at Berger:

"Are you coming along?"

Berger felt a little confused as he nodded assent.

"Yes, why not?"

On the way to the restaurant, they did not exchange a single word. They walked side by side like two conspirators. Not until they had reached the place and were seated did the stranger speak:

"I know who you are, but you don't know me. Perhaps I may as well confess now as later that my name is Rognaas."

They shook hands over the table, briefly and silently.

Half a minute passed before Berger became conscious of his own surprise.

"How in the world can you know who I am?"

Rognaas smiled faintly.

"At one time we worked in the same city," he said. "You were in the post-office and I was connected with one of the banks. Everybody does not go to the bank, but most of us have to visit the post-office now and then."

Berger flushed deeply and looked at the other one in a helpless fashion.

"Yes," he said. "Yes . . ."

The smile of Rognaas became more subtle. At the same time, a searching look came into his eyes.

"On top of it," he said, "I made an enemy of one of your colleagues for your sake . . . a sulky, red-haired fellow named Lydersen."

Berger's surprise increased.

"You knew Lydersen?"

"I did, and I found that he was very fond of playing the hero on some occasions."

This brought him a questioning and disturbed glance from Berger, who asked:

"At my expense?"

"Exactly. I did what I could to strip him of his pretensions. But it was not very effective. He *must* be a hero and would hear nothing about having acted like an hysterical idiot."

"Do you really mean what you say?"

Berger's voice trembled with pleasurable but still faltering emotion.

Rognaas looked back at him with sudden seriousness.

"Of course, I do," he said. "We live only once."

Then Berger's glance fell to the table. During the silence that followed, he played unconsciously with his spoon.

"Those are the very words I have used," he said quietly.

There was something in his tone that interested Rognaas.

"And you have suffered a great deal on that account?"

When Berger merely nodded, Rognaas went on:

"I know that once he was promoted ahead of you. But after that?"

Berger straightened up, moved by a touch of rebellion against his own fate.

"I stay where I am," he said. "I am nothing but a clerk."

"And Lydersen?"

"He is a division head of the first class."

"Promoted again, then?"

"Yes."

Berger gave him a timid glance, and Rognaas shook his head as if unable to understand.

"We human beings are a lot of strange beasts," he said. "Those who act sensibly we call cowards, and we reward the idiots."

The watchful, suspicious look of Berger's turned into one of pure surprise.

"How did all this come to make such an impression on you?"

Rognaas was surprised in his turn by that question. A somewhat startled expression appeared on his firmly outlined face. After a while he replied pensively:

"I really don't know. But perhaps the reason was that I could never bear the man."

A little later they began to talk about Kvisthus, and Berger said:

"That was a different kind of man . . . a thoroughly fine man . . . and it was a rank pity that he had to die."

Rognaas shook his head.

"I didn't know him at all."

"He was of about the same age as I . . . slender, with rather light hair."

When Rognaas continued to say nothing, Berger added:

"He was the only friend I ever had . . . after I grew up."

Then Rognaas looked up:

"Was he married?"

"Yes, and he had a little boy."

Rognaas shook his head in commiseration.

"That's a pity," he said. "And how are the widow and the boy getting along?"

Berger shrugged his shoulders significantly.

"Of course, they got a small pension."

A moment later he remarked guiltily in a low voice:

"I ought to have looked after them, but I didn't."

There was a pause. Both of them had finished their coffee, but they remained sitting there as if tied together by the sadness of their conversation. Rognaas rested his head in one of his hands and gazed down at the table.

"I understand what it means," he said. "I also had a friend who is now dead."

Berger studied him with sympathy, but the other one did not look up.

"Recently?" Berger asked.

"It happened a year ago. He was killed in an accident. I was with him at the time, and I can never get over it. That is really what has made me so nervous."

The monotonous way in which he spoke, dropping one word at a time, had a depressing effect on Berger. He should have like to ask how it happened, but his courage failed him. He couldn't do it. Instead he said:

"This is perhaps what has brought us together."

When Rognaas lowered his hand and looked up in surprise, Berger confessed with a wry smile:

"I came here two nights to look for you."

"For me?"

"I did. It may sound ridiculous, but it is true."

"When was that?"

"A week after our first meeting."

Then Rognaas managed to smile again. It was a sly smile that shattered the heavy mood that had descended on them.

"*I* was here the three first nights," he said.

Then they looked at each other and laughed outright.

2

WHEN Berger went home that night, it struck him that both he and Rognaas had found a compensation for the loss of their dead friends. This compensation was not complete, of course. Rognaas could not be to Berger what Kvisthus had been . . . no more than he could hope to fill the place of the unknown man entirely. A friendship formed in mature years can never assume the aspect of inevitability attaching to the friendships of youth. There is always something more reserved about the former.

"And yet," he thought, "it may be of a more serious nature at this time. It may turn out a more self-conscious friendship. We are two grown-up and lonely people who suffer from our loneliness and have a need of each other."

Temporarily he said nothing about it to Helen. He was held back by a fear of revealing what had not yet taken firm root and might prove unstable in the end. Nor did he have any desire to bring Rognaas to his home. He wished to have him to himself, just as Helen had women friends who were practically unknown to him.

Rognaas did not ask Berger to his home either. Neither of them knew definitely where the other one lived. They continued to meet in restaurants. Now and then they took a good, long walk together, but neither one of them ever saw the other one to his door. It did not seem to occur to them to do so.

Often they would spend a long time together without saying a word. But always, even in the midst of a crowd, they had an intense consciousness of each other's presence.

In the end, however, it became impossible for Berger to keep this new friendship a secret. He had been accustomed to spend most of his free time at home, and Helen noticed the change in his habits, even though he stayed out only a couple of times a week and never came home later than twelve.

One day she wondered about it, and he told her everything, beginning with the first time they met. He felt embarrassed when he started, but little by little this feeling passed, as it generally did when something interested him greatly, and soon he was talking with a great deal of warmth.

Helen listened to him with a certain air of suspicion that bothered him. But when he was through, she looked at him for a long time with a great deal of concern.

"I hope it will not prove a disappointment," she said at last.

Her attitude of resigned reserve caused him to blush.

"Why should it?"

She was supporting her head with one hand, and her eyes were turned down.

"Because that seems to be our destiny," she replied with a bitter note in her voice that hurt him, but that also goaded him into a protest.

"Why are you so bitter?" he asked.

"Because we have good reason to feel bitter... both of us."

"Yes," he said, "perhaps we have. But it does not help us. And if I can bear my disappointments, you should be able to bear yours."

Then she looked up with something like hostility in her attention.

"What do you mean by that?"

He rose without answering and walked back and forth for a while. But when she repeated her question, he turned to her again, a little more composed by that time.

"I can tell you," he said, "but you must not be offended if I do. The point of the whole thing is this. It is my self-respect that is hurt, but in you it is nothing but your ambition."

She pooh-poohed scornfully.

"Ambition?"

He nodded once, quickly.

"Yes . . . your ambition on my behalf."

His words startled her. A moment later she asked thoughtfully:

"And have you no ambition on your own behalf?"

"Yes," he replied, "but it does not come first."

3

IN the course of that same winter it was just Berger's checked ambition that suffered a new wound. Something happened that brought back to him all his former suffering and made it as vivid and meaningless as it had been seven years earlier.

One evening in January he reached the depot at the end of a trip. As it was Wednesday, he was to meet Rognaas, this having become a habit with them. It was a very ordinary day, with no suggestion of expectancy or sensational possibilities about it. The weather was gloomy, as is mostly the case in January, and rather saddening on that account, with a starless sky from which occasional half-melted snow flakes seemed to be dropping pensively.

Berger turned up his coat collar and felt quite brisk, as generally happened when there was light snow and he was dressed to meet it. Before he went to the restaurant, it occurred to him to take a look at the evening paper that was displayed outside the adjoining branch office for the handling of newspaper mail. There was nothing of particular interest in it, and he let his eyes run down the columns without paying attention to anything but the headlines. But he stopped at a notice headed "The Postal Service" and began to read, although not yet seriously interested.

Suddenly he took his pipe out of his mouth with an angular movement like that of an automaton. There he stood as if paralyzed, staring at the few lines in small type which announced that Lydersen had been made a postmaster.

He had to make an effort to get away from there. In a state of dumb apathy, without any feeling of hatred, envy, or bitterness, he turned and walked away. He collided with several fellow-citizens without asking their pardon and almost without being aware of what happened.

In front of the restaurant he was halted by Rognaas, just as he was about to pass by it.

"Have you forgotten the way in?"

Berger looked up in confusion. Then he recalled both what he was to do that night and what they had discussed on a previous occasion. That latter memory made his face burn. Without any attempt at dissimulation or restraint, he looked Rognaas straight in the face with a helpless and anything but heroic expression.

"Have you seen that they have made Lydersen a postmaster?"

Rognaas nodded.

"Yes," he said. "But let us get inside. We'll be drenched if we stay here."

Berger submitted passively to his guidance. When they had found a table, he calmed down somewhat, but he felt peculiarly humble and hurt. He tried to smile at Rognaas, and this smile was meant to appear gay.

"Do you read about the post-office also?"

Rognaas regarded him with a cautious and carefully restrained sympathy.

"It happens," he said. "Especially when the paper is as stupid as it was this evening."

A little later he said:

"I can well understand that you feel this deeply. But this time you have at least not been passed over."

Berger sat up straight, with a slow movement, as if he had just waked up.

"What do you mean?"

There was a suggestion of rebuff in his attitude, but Rognaas did not permit himself to be intimidated by it.

"I mean," he said, "that this time Lydersen may have had a certain right to his new position. I assume that he was old enough to expect a promotion of that kind. In other words, I suppose that he was the oldest applicant. Am I right?"

"I don't know. But even then?"

Rognaas went on, a little disturbed by this unexpected resistance.

"Then," he said, "the man was entitled to the

position under existing circumstances . . . even, as I see it, if he had never been guilty of that notorious piece of heroism. In other words, this promotion is not the result of . . . what happened eight years ago."

Berger looked at him in the same obstinate fashion.

"Not except in so far . . ." he said.

"Except in so far?"

Berger's thin and boyish face colored slightly.

"Except in so far as I was prevented from being an applicant . . . prevented exactly by what happened eight years ago. It was that happening that gave him his seniority."

Rognaas regarded him with astonishment.

"You mean that you would have applied . . . under normal conditions."

"Yes."

"But why didn't you do it anyhow? That old story is probably forgotten by now."

Berger smiled an acrid smile.

"Thank you," he said, "that would be nice, if it were so. And the day it happens, then I shall begin to compete with Lydersen in earnest. But I do not care to expose myself to a new snub like the one I got before."

After a brief pause he went on:

"I am not a trouble-maker. And I don't wish to become one. For that reason I have often wished that Lydersen were the older one of us two. Then I should have been spared a great many humiliations."

But Rognaas rejoined:

"That sounds all right. But it is barely possible that your bitterness would have been far more corrosive in character without the outlet provided for it by those very humiliations."

"I don't understand."

The words were spoken with an excitement that caused Rognaas to hesitate.

"Perhaps I am mistaken," he said. "I meant only that a hidden wound is apt to be more dangerous than one that shows openly . . . that the former is more likely to become infected."

This idea startled Berger, and he pondered it for a long time.

"I think you are right," he admitted at last. "I believe that is true."

Shortly afterward he rose halfway with an embarrassed glance at Rognaas.

"I feel better now," he said, "and I think I ought to go home. My wife has undoubtedly seen the newspaper too. And I like to have it over."

Then Rognaas asked a little timidly:

"How has she taken it?"

Berger shrugged his shoulders.

"A little more heavily than I," he answered casually.

Rognaas gave a start.

"More heavily than you?"

"Yes."

"But why should she? That is more than I can understand."

Berger looked up at him quickly.

"Because she has never faced a gun. Because she has never had a single second to decide whether she preferred to live or die."

He turned red with mortification the moment he had spoken. And his own disturbance infected the man who had asked the question. It had suddenly led to a confession unforeseen by either one of them, and both of them were troubled by it.

BERGER was driven by his disquietude to make earnest of his decision to go home. It caused them to part rather abruptly, as if their meeting had been interrupted. And they did not go out together. Rognaas stayed behind when Berger left.

On his way home Berger suffered from a sort of

morning-after remorse because he had been too frank in showing how much he resented his own humiliation. It served, however, to neutralize the nervousness with which the thought of his home had filled him. He knew this to be the case, but it tended nevertheless to make him contemptuously angry with himself.

"I hope he doesn't think that I was prompted by envy," he thought. "I am not envious. On the contrary, I wish Lydersen every possible success. But I don't want him to be successful at my expense. I want it least of all in his case, for it is his fault that things are what they are. If Kvisthus and I had been alone that evening, no one would have reproached me for keeping alive."

And all his ancient bitterness against Lydersen rose into a new flood-tide.

"And in reality he has nothing at all to be proud of," Berger declared to himself. "A mere accident settled the matter. If I had been in his place that evening, and had been taken by surprise as he was, and if he had had time to think, as I had, then our positions would be reversed today. He was too stupid to think fast enough," Berger added, "and so he let himself be knocked on the head like an ox."

Once more he became filled with a bitter yearning to get even with Lydersen.

"If I only knew how it could be done," he thought. "All I know is that I must score against him some time, sooner or later. Things cannot stay as they are to the end of my life. That would be unendurable. But it helps at least that Rognaas is taking my side. I do not stand entirely alone. I was lucky to run into him that night. And I hope I didn't drive him away again tonight. He appeared somewhat reserved. It looked almost as if he wished me to be in the wrong.

"And what I said about Helen," he went on, feeling ill at ease. "I really should not have mentioned it. And for a long time now the situation between us has been much improved. I should have told him that.—But I hate to think of how she will take this matter tonight.—What will she say?—When I get home before she expects me, she will understand that I have seen the news. That is, if she has seen it herself. Which I hope. For then I shall at least miss the trouble of telling her."

His uneasiness and nervousness increased as he approached the street where they lived. A sense of guilty dejection choked him, and with a sort of grim humor he said to himself:

"I feel almost as I did that time. It is almost as if they had robbed me of the money all over again."

This way of looking at it helped a little and gave him more courage. It furnished him with an answer that ought to stop her if she was inclined to relapse into her old unreasonable attitude. He had been robbed once, and he had been punished for it. There was no reason why he should expect to be punished for it again.

Nevertheless he hoped that Leif already had gone to bed, so that he did not have to renew a memory which the boy might have lost.

BUT WHEN he got home, it was the boy who opened the door for him. He smiled in his usual way, as a good pal, so that Berger was sure that at least she had said nothing to the boy. Berger began to talk at once, in a somewhat forced manner perhaps, but so that they were still eagerly concerned with each other when they entered. And he went on talking after having given Helen a friendly nod.

She stared at him in wide-eyed astonishment, but she went right on with her sewing.

It suddenly made him more nervous. It gave him a panicky feeling that she was withdrawing herself, drawing away from him and all that referred to him.

This must not happen, and so he rubbed his hands and spoke straight to her:

"It's pretty rough outside tonight."

Then she looked up.

"You are early tonight?"

He smiled uneasily, knowing that it must make him look silly.

"Yes, I am," he said. "Aren't you glad of it?"

Again that astonished expression appeared on her face. It was clear, thank heaven, that she did not know where she had him. Then she repeated what he had said about the weather . . . on purpose evidently, as if she were feeling her way.

"Rough?" she said. Then she hesitated a moment before deciding to go on: "I thought that today you would be hot and cold by turns."

He looked back at her coldly, hoping to check her.

"Why should I? I don't know of anything in the world that could give me a guilty conscience."

She turned a shade paler and raised her eyebrows.

"Oh, you don't? Well, well . . . then there is nothing to discuss."

The boy looked in a puzzled way from one to the other.

"What's up now?"

Neither one of them answered, but both showed that something must be wrong.

"What is it, Father?"

The anxiety in the boy's voice hurt Berger, but he merely shook his head.

"Nothing at all, my boy. Nothing that you can understand . . . yet. You had better go to bed. It is after ten."

And he patted the boy's hair in bidding him good-night, bending his head slightly backward before he let it go.

"Have you learned your lessons?"

The boy laughed with relief when he caught the casualness of his father's tone.

"Oh, yes!" And then he added mischievously: "Perhaps you would like to hear?"

His father laughed too.

"No," he said, "not after ten o'clock."

Then the boy said good-night to both of them, affectionately as always. Berger stood looking after him for a while. When the door of the boy's room had been closed, he said in a fatigued and saddened voice:

"It would seem to me that at least we might keep him outside. He is nothing but a boy now and his head is full of hero-worship. When he grows older, he will be able to understand what I tell him about it. And I don't want him, too, to be disappointed in me."

Helen made no reply, and he began to walk about the room uneasily. At last she put away her sewing and looked up with a sigh.

"Well," she said, "now I can say to you what you once said to me: Congratulations on account of Lydersen!"

He turned red in the face and shrugged his shoulders.

"Heavens!" he said. "That's not much of a position . . . nothing but a fourth-rate post-office."

Then she asked sarcastically:

"Perhaps you wouldn't have taken it even?"

"Oh, yes," he replied honestly, "I would."

A little later she asked again:

"Did you tell Rognaas?"

"He had read it himself. But he thought I had no cause to feel hurt on that account. If Lydersen was the oldest applicant, he was entitled to the position, of course. And Rognaas reproached me a little for not having applied myself. He thought that that old story was forgotten . . . as far as I am concerned."

Her voice was unsteady when she asked:

"Do you really think so yourself?"

He shook his head.

"No, I don't. On the contrary."

The paper was lying on the table, and she spread it out, found the notice, and read it over again . . . the Lord alone knowing how many times she had read it before. Berger stood watching her guiltily. Minutes went by, and she could not take her eyes away from it. He began to feel offended and irritated. At last she turned the page slowly. At the same time she looked up and said wearily and dejectedly:

"Yes, it might have been you."

"Yes," he retorted, "but it might also have been Kvisthus."

"And Lydersen might have been Kvisthus."

"Yes, and he might also have been me. If conditions had been different. But no one seems to think of that."

She pondered this for a while. There was something in his firm gentleness that disarmed her and filled her with sympathy in spite of her bitterness.

"It's a pity anyhow," she said, "that it should be as it is."

Berger went over to her, full of gratitude. Standing behind her, he stroked her hair tenderly, while she sat staring straight ahead . . . evidently without seeing anything at all.

"Yes," he said, "it is strange to be alive, and yet to be denied the full rights of a living human being . . . merely because I am alive."

4

NEXT Saturday Berger and Rognaas were to meet again. Berger appeared in a rather depressed mood. He was embarrassed at having bared his feelings too freely during their previous meeting. But his regrets were wasted. Rognaas did not appear at all.

As late as ten o'clock Berger still nourished a hope of seeing his friend enter. Thus he had sat there one whole hour, his eyes on the door, his mind full of restless impatience to be done with the embarrassment of their initial greetings. After ten he gave up the door and began to look at his watch instead. The first quarter passed. Soon it was half past ten. Eleven o'clock was drawing near. Then he realized with a sense of profound dejection that his friend would not show up.

He went home utterly nonplussed, and he walked far out of his way in order to make the time pass, so that Helen might not notice anything and begin to ask questions.

"Nothing is wrong, I am sure," he tried to console himself. "There is no reason to think that he is sick. Something has turned up to keep him away."

Berger brooded a good deal during the four days he had to wait until it was Wednesday again. He seemed to be missing something . . . to have been cheated out of something.

At last that impatiently expected evening came around, and he hurried off to their meeting. He seemed to know in advance what would happen, and it made him uneasy and nervous. His forebodings proved warranted. Rognaas did not appear that time either.

Then Berger began to give the problem more serious thought. But no matter how he might turn it and twist it, no matter how he looked at it, he came back to the same definite conclusion.

"Rognaas must be sick. It is stupid of me not to have made sure of his address so that I could call on him."

On this occasion, as on the previous one, he chose a roundabout route on his way home, but now he did not do so in order to escape any inquiries. He wanted to be alone with his problem. And he wanted to get to the bottom of another, later problem: How much did Rognaas really mean to him?

Up one street and down another he walked through the snow of that bitter January night without being aware of his surroundings. Nor did these matter, for in reality he was never anywhere but within himself. And there he felt more lonely than at any time during the long, barren years that preceded his first meeting with Rognaas. His despair approached almost what he felt that evening when he left the police station knowing that Kvisthus must die.

"Oh, yes, Kvisthus . . . ," he thought. "How they spoiled my sorrow and made me feel ashamed of missing you! I did miss you, and my sorrow was deep indeed. But it would have been more pure if all that filth had not been flung at me."

But Rognaas was not Kvisthus, and if he lost him, he would feel that loss in a different, less exalted fashion. Kvisthus was light of complexion and slight of build. He was kindly and jolly. Rognaas was tall and muscular, with a serious, somewhat reserved face. He was really better-looking, but not so easy to approach.

"He will never be what Kvisthus was to me," Berger thought. "But I really need a different kind of friend now, and Rognaas is just what I need him to be."

Finally he shook himself free of those thoughts and went home.

"It's of no use for me to get tragical and solemn," he thought. "I have not lost him yet, and it will be Saturday again three days from now. Then he will come perhaps, and we can go on as we began."

5

THAT Saturday, at nine o'clock, Rognaas was waiting for him in front of the restaurant. Berger caught sight of him while still far down the street, and the feeling of uneasiness with which he met him was quite different from what he had expected. Their previous talk was entirely forgotten. Instead he felt that slightly embarrassed, slightly constrained depression which friends sometimes feel when they suddenly meet after many years or after a long journey.

And he noticed quickly that his friend felt the same thing. After their first greeting, they avoided looking at each other.

Rognaas dug a hole in the snow with his rubber and studied it with feigned interest while he said:

"I have often thought that it might be pleasant some time to come together in some other place than this tedious restaurant."

Berger regarded him doubtfully. And at that moment it struck him that his friend looked pale and thin. He must certainly have been sick.

"Ye-es," he replied guardedly.

Then Rognaas looked as if he come to a decision.

"I thought that perhaps we might go to my home."

Berger made no objection. On the contrary, it filled him with happy and excited suspense. And so they went.

Rognaas lived in the northern part of the city, and so they took the Ullevaal Road in that direction. For a while they walked in silence. But soon Berger couldn't bear it any longer, and he said:

"I was afraid I had scared you away with all that talk about my own affairs."

Rognaas gave him a quick glance.

"Why should you feel that way?" And with the casualness of a mere shoulder-shrug he added: "At times it does us good to hear about other people's troubles. It keeps us from thinking of our own all the time."

"Have you been sick then?"

Rognaas answered curtly, without looking at his friend:

"Not exactly. But I have not been well."

He gave an impression of not caring to talk about it. It made Berger recall what Rognaas once had told him about his insomnia and the loss of his friend by an accident. Those were matters he could understand, and they walked the rest of the way in silence.

ROGNAAS lived on the second floor, above a grocery store. His room was a very large one, but so simply furnished that it looked bare. It surprised Berger, but he forgot all about it as soon as Rognaas had made him sit down at the table, placing whiskey and soda in front of him.

They tasted their high-balls in silence and felt a little out of touch when thus suddenly they found themselves seated face to face, all by themselves. Their first attempts at talk were cautious and groping on both sides. Then Rognaas rose unexpectedly from the table. He went over to a shelf and picked up a pipe. Then he made another trip in search of tobacco, and a third one to find matches. At last he sat down and began to fill his pipe with hands that clearly showed his nervousness. A moment later he rose again and remained standing. Finally he put down the pipe, unlighted as it was when he picked it up.

"No!" he said.

Berger looked up startled and met a troubled and excited expression that made his heart stand still. With a choking sense of fear he asked:

"Is anything the matter?"

Rognaas leaned forward and placed both hands on the table. His face was dreadfully white, and he shivered as if stricken with ague. Then it seemed as if he pulled his entire being together into one tremendous exertion of will power.

"Yes," he said slowly and with heavy emphasis on every word, "I avoided you purposely during the last two weeks. The reason was that *I know who killed Kvisthus.*"

Berger had risen noiselessly. During the few seconds that their eyes met fully, the silence that fell between them seemed fraught with madness.

Then the truth struck Berger in a lightning-like flash . . . logical, incontrovertible, and overwhelming. And he asked hoarsely:

"Was it *you?*"

Without changing his position, and with the same violent effort, Rognaas answered:

"No . . . but it was I who took the money."

Another moment of surcharged silence followed. Then, without thought of what he was doing, as if moved by an instinctive fury, Berger took his hand from the table and struck at the white face in front of him with all his power. Rognaas staggered under the blow, but a moment later he stood immobile as before, leaning on the table, his eyes firmly fixed on those of Berger.

And Berger drew back a step, dropped his own eyes, and let his hand sink to his side, feeling thwarted and stripped of all will.

"No," he said brokenly, "it doesn't matter any longer."

Then he slid down on the chair, drooped forward over the table, buried his head in his arms and began suddenly to cry . . . wildly, beyond all control. It was not the kind of crying that makes the tears flow freely, but rather a sobbing, heart-breaking wail.

Without saying a word, Rognaas sat down at the other end of the table, facing him. A sort of congealed calm had appeared on his face . . . an expression of gloomy expectancy.

After a while he said:

"If you will keep calm, I shall tell you all about it."

Then Berger straightened up. He looked at the other man, but could no longer catch his eyes.

"Calm?" he repeated in despair. "Calm?"

When Rognaas still failed to meet his glance, he drifted over to the window, overwhelmed by anger and pain. When he turned around at last, Rognaas sat staring at the floor as before. On the table in front of him stood the bottles and glasses, their presence having lost all meaning in the meantime. It seemed as if he had been sitting there through a whole eternity. And in the midst of Berger's suffering, the sight of him had the effect of an ancient memory of happier days.

It stirred him so strongly that he had to turn away again. He seated himself by the window and looked down at the street without seeing anything at all. And little by little the storm and the tumult within him died out. A heavy, rebellious hardness took hold of him instead. And it hurt him in another, more profound manner. It showed him the necessity of what was happening that night. But it also served to expose the horror of having his latest, his only friend involved in it. It revealed the impossibility of any vindication. It was final and terrifying as death itself.

He tore himself away from those thoughts and rose.

Rognaas sat as before, his face white and rigid. Berger stood looking at him for a while. And then it was no longer an enemy of his that sat there. It was a man who had been guilty of dreadful deeds, but who also had given him hours of sheltered intimacy.

Without taking his eyes away from that man, Berger went back to his former place at the table and sat down quietly.

"Tell me all about it," he said.

It was a plea rather than a command. And when Rognaas raised his head with an air of suppressed emotion, Berger asked:

"Who killed Kvisthus?"

The corners of Rognaas' mouth trembled slightly, with a suggestion of helplessness. There was a wounded expression in his eyes, and he hesitated a moment before he answered.

"It was he . . . the man who died," he said. "But he didn't want to do it. He had no such intention at all. We didn't mean anything to happen as it did."

He stopped abruptly. While his glance fled that of Berger again, he reached nervously for the highball and took a long, eager drink, the hand that held the glass trembling visibly. Then he replaced the glass on the table and pushed it away with an expression of intense bitterness.

"We did not mean to kill any one!" he said.

It came in a violent and tortured burst. He had to rise and move about.

But suddenly he turned back and looked straight at Berger.

"We have had a worse time of it than you," he said. "Suppose even that you *had* stolen the money ... what is that in comparison with having killed a man?"

Berger had a feeling of being placed against a wall.

"And yet you defended me?"

Rognaas looked away again and quieted down a little.

"Yes," he confessed, "partly to lessen my own guilt, and partly out of gratitude because *I* did not have to kill."

"But you didn't mean to do it?"

"Yes, my mind was made up. And this was something I had to make clear, not only to others, but to you personally. You think it was an accident that made us meet in the restaurant. Yes, but it was no accident that made me sit down at your table."

"You did it on purpose?"

"Yes, on purpose."

Berger gaped at him.

"And the next time . . . down by the depot?"

Rognaas still avoided his look. But he nodded affirmatively.

"Yes," he said, "I came down there that night to find you."

"And after that? All those other nights we had together?"

There was fear in Berger's voice . . . a fear of losing something that had grown precious to him. But the reply of Rognaas reassured him.

"Then I couldn't stay away any longer," he said. "I felt so lonely. But it hurt me deeply to hear you tell about the subsequent results of that event."

Berger was seized by a timid sort of pity, and he asked:

"Is that why we are here tonight?"

Rognaas nodded.

"Yes," he replied. "And because I can't stand it

any longer. It was different at first. There was a time when I felt that we belonged together just because we had suffered from the same happening . . . although in different ways." He looked searchingly at Berger: "I meant no offense by saying that."

Berger shook his head helplessly.

"No, I understand. And I can understand all the rest, too."

Rognaas continued to observe him.

"That I could be guilty of a crime also?"

But this Berger denied vehemently.

"No, no!" he broke out. "You are an ordinary decent human being."

Rognaas stared at the floor again, and his face twitched.

"That is just what both of us were. And that is the most terrible thing of all."

After a brief silence Berger asked:

"Who was the other one?"

Rognaas shook his head in refusal.

"You won't tell?"

Rognaas shook his head in the same way as before.

Then Berger asked apprehensively:

"Did I know him?"

"No, you had only seen him twice."

"When did I see him the second time?"

"At the hospital."

"At the hospital?"

Rognaas hesitated a good deal before he looked up.

"Can you remember that they brought in a cyclist who had been hurt in an accident and whose wounds were washed and bandaged?"

Berger thought rapidly.

"I do," he said. "And so it was he?"

"Yes, it was the only way he could explain the wound inflicted by Lydersen."

Berger stared at him in surprise.

"I don't understand," he said. "The damaged cycle was right there."

Rognaas met his look with nervous uneasiness.

"Of course," he said. "He had to arrange the whole thing carefully, and so he went smash right on the street in order to be sure of witnesses."

Upset by his memories, he turned away and walked restlessly over to the window. Berger sat looking after him, overwhelmed and terrified by what he had heard.

"Please tell me," he asked hoarsely. "Tell me all about it."

And Rognaas replied without checking his slow, restive drifting about:

"Let me calm down a little first. This is a perfect hell to me."

Then Berger settled down to wait quietly and patiently. He felt upset and paralyzed, and his very body seemed to be sore, as if he had received a violent blow or had suffered a fall.

"So this is the miracle I have been expecting," he thought. "O Lord . . . I wish You would take it back again!"

6

FINALLY Rognaas calmed down enough to begin his story. He was again seated as before, with the table between himself and Berger. He rested his head against his right hand. His voice was firm again, almost cold, but he did not look up at all.

"I shall begin with the beginning," he said. "And the beginning is not the hold-up, but the reasons for it . . . what made us do such a thing. Originally we were just what you said . . . ordinary, decent human beings. I shall not bother you with details. They would not interest you. Of course, I understand that you would prefer to hear about the deed itself, but it is necessary that you should also know all these other circumstances."

Suddenly he looked up.

"I don't mean these circumstances to serve as an excuse for us," he said, "but they will at least help to explain."

Berger nodded, sick with suspense and eagerness to get at the main event. And Rognaas resumed. Externally he appeared cold and self-controlled, but in reality he was deeply agitated and struggling against an intense inner resistance.

"We had been speculating together," he said. "At one time both of us lived here in Oslo, and after both of us had moved to the other city we used to see each other at least once a week. We speculated together, as I said, and like most people, we lost. We did not only lose what we ourselves possessed. Like many others, we did not merely lose certain shadowy sums owned by no one, because they never had any real existence. The terrible thing was that we lost money belonging to others. Both of us had money entrusted to us—I in the bank, he in a private business. And in order to recoup, we began to borrow in a small way, very cautiously. And the end of it was that we had a shortage of about twenty thousand kroner. Then we were frightened in earnest. We borrowed all we could, and we stopped our speculations. But that didn't help very much. That autumn, when the hold-up took place, we still faced a common shortage of twelve thousand kroner, but it appeared in only one account . . . his, namely . . . because it was easier for him to manipulate matters so that discovery was delayed. But, of course, that situation couldn't last for ever. Some day the fatal hour must strike not only for us, but for those who were in any way connected with us. Both of us belonged to good families, but with no wealth on either side. As the year approached its end, we grew more and more nervous. It seemed pretty clear that we must be exposed at New Year, when the books were balanced. It meant criminal prosecution and imprisonment. And now you will perhaps understand how we could resort to such a madly desperate attempt. We could see no other way out of it, and our faculty of moral judgment and resistance must have ceased functioning entirely . . . or so it seems to me now at least. It was paralyzed by fear."

He remained silent for a long while, his face reflecting the dread memories that were passing through his mind.

Berger moved uneasily on his chair.

"But the post-office?" he wondered. "Why did you choose the post-office for your purpose?"

Rognaas hesitated before he answered.

"That was almost accidental," he said. "It happened by an accident that may strike you as ridiculous. We read in the paper about a man in Copenhagen who robbed a post-office in order to get money for making a home when he married. In broad daylight he entered the post-office with a gun in his hand and forced the employees to hand over the cash money. As soon as he had got it, he calmly walked out."

"But was he not caught?"

Rognaas smiled a weary and indulgent smile.

"Yes," he said, "he was caught. A small girl saw him and happened to recognize him. Afterward he told them that he undoubtedly was the most badly frightened man in that office. But we thought that, with better precautions, we might easily make a success of the same thing. As far as we were concerned, it was a romantic and hazardous adventure rather than an attempt at robbery accompanied by murder. Perhaps we were carried away by our own childlike lack of experience. It never occurred to us that a life might have to be sacrificed."

"But you must have been well acquainted with

conditions in the post-office. You picked the right time, and you were able to find the rear entrance, which is not an easy matter."

"What knowledge I had I had gathered from occasional remarks by Lydersen. You see, we lived for a couple of years in the same boarding-house."

"And were you not scared by the dreadful risk you took?"

Rognaas shook his head.

"No," he replied. "We figured out that we need take no risk at all. And in a way we were right. The case has remained unsolved until this very day."

Berger stared at him with uncomprehending amazement.

"But how could you figure that out?"

"Oh, it was easy. We started with the premise that no one on earth would ever dream of suspecting us two."

"How could you be so sure of that?"

"Ask rather whether there was any reason for us *not* to be sure of that? If you should blow open a safe here in Oslo tonight and not leave a single clue behind, do you think any human being would ever think of you in connection with such a crime?"

For a moment Berger was taken aback, struck by the absolute logic of that argument.

"No, you are right," he muttered. "I never thought of that."

"No. And no one else has done so either. All we had to do, then, was to put over our coup without being recognized. Then we had to disappear without leaving a trace behind. This part we thought the most difficult. At any rate, it cost us a lot of hard thinking. Before we made up our minds, we had to test the effectiveness of our plans in the face of all possible emergencies. And the result proved that they were well laid. It was the main action that went wrong for us."

"You had not counted on any resistance?"

"No . . . and not with the possibility that we ourselves might become panic-stricken."

The voice of Berger was unsteady:

"And you did?"

Rognaas breathed heavily and rose.

"Yes," he said, "we did."

He walked back and forth a couple of times while Berger sat with his back turned to him and waited without moving a muscle. Then Rognaas returned to his seat, his features rigid and stern as he asked:

"Do you think that Rognaas, the robber and murderer, is a very dreadful person?"

Berger sat staring at him intently, incapable of answering.

"Tell more," he asked. His throat was dry, and his suspense made it impossible for him to carry his reasoning beyond the naked and palpable facts of the case.

Rognaas raised his eyebrows nervously. Then he folded his arms across his breast and looked straight ahead, his face bent slightly forward.

"You know what happened at the post-office," he said. "Or rather, you imagine that you know it. For it did not happen in accordance with the reconstruction of the events in the newspapers."

Resentment caused Berger to wrinkle his forehead.

"Do you mean to say that we exaggerated?"

Rognaas shook his head in disavowal.

"Not at all. Everything was straight as far as you were concerned. And to a certain extent that could also be said of Lydersen's part. It is the 'murder' I am thinking of. For it was not a murder. It was an accidental homicide."

"Accidental?"

"Well, do you still think that we meant to kill anybody?"

"Yes, I still think that you would have shot me."

The stubborn tone of that answer caused Rognaas to pause.

"We'll get to that point later," he said. "In the meantime something decisive had happened... something that made our crime ever so much more serious... something that made it necessary for us to escape at any price."

He paused again, and both of them looked paler. Berger drew back a little timidly.

"Are you thinking of Kvisthus?" he asked in a low voice.

"I am. We had him lying there behind us, and we didn't know whether he was dead or alive."

"How did it happen?"

"I hardly know. I saw only that those two unexpectedly collided right before my eyes. It looked as if Kvisthus... without suspecting any particular danger... had got in front of my friend in order to stop him. Later I learned that he had struck the gun aside. He got the blow in return. How hard it was, I don't know, but it went home, and with unfortunate results. Kvisthus had the cash box under his arm. He stumbled and fell flat against the stone floor without being able to lessen the force of it. That was the 'murder.' We had no time to look at him. We had to move quickly and get away at any price. Of course, we might have turned tail at once. But we didn't. We did not come to any agreement, and now I can't understand why we didn't. Unless it was because we both felt . . . without realizing it clearly . . . that now we had to get something out of it."

Berger regarded him sceptically.

"Are you really sure that that was the way he was killed?"

Rognaas nodded curtly.

"I am," he said. "I think it agrees with the story printed in the papers. And you could probably see for yourself. He was lying with his face against the floor, and his forehead had been crushed in. Otherwise he showed nothing but the mark of a quite insignificant blow."

Berger rubbed his hands together nervously.

"Yes, you are right," he said. "And then Lydersen appeared?"

"Not exactly. It was we who appeared to him. And he was far more surprised than Kvisthus. And much more scared. It was no heroism that made him fight, and not for a moment did he think of the money. It may sound silly, but it was that fact which made him most unbearable to me afterward."

Berger shook his head uncomprehendingly.

"Why did he fight at all then?"

"Out of sheer fright. He was seized by a panic as complete as our own."

"Was that the reason?"

"Yes, just that was the reason!"

A feverish apprehension stirred both of them. They were approaching the crucial point . . . what had happened between themselves.

Berger sighed heavily.

"And then you came over to me," he said.

"Yes . . . then we came over to you. But if you hadn't opened the door, we should probably not have taken the time to look for you. I had already tried one door in vain. And we had to get away. Then he called to me . . . for he was the only one who saw you . . . that you were in there. Then I ran after you. And the rest you know."

Berger turned halfway around and looked flurriedly at Rognaas.

"Would you have fired?" he demanded.

Rognaas leaned his forehead against the palms of his hands and looked down with an expression of great weariness before he answered.

"I have asked myself that question," he said.

"And what answer did you give yourself?"

The suspense of both was unnatural and irrational.

Then Rognaas raised his face.

"I should prefer to answer no," he said. "But in order to be honest I must instead answer: Yes, I should have fired. You hesitated such a long time, and we couldn't spare a second . . . considering the crimes of which we already had become guilty. When I recall my own excitement, and my feverish eagerness to get out, I cannot understand why I did not shoot you."

"Did you think of the noise a shot would have made?"

"No, I didn't think at all. I was too excited by what we had already done."

"And it never occurred to you that I might have raised an outcry?"

Rognaas shook his head in a way that showed his inner disturbance.

"Both of us were past thinking. And I don't remember how we got out. All I remember is that we drove off without any light, and that we followed the route we had practised by sheer instinct. But now, when I have worked myself back into all this, you must not interrupt me so frequently. I am no longer telling this for your sake alone. I am also telling it for my own sake."

He rose restlessly and began to stroll around the room in a nervous struggle for self-control. Berger waited in a suspense that made him feel sick, but he said nothing to disturb him. He watched Rognaas light a cigaret, absent-mindedly and with hands that trembled visibly. Then he picked up his own pipe, but found the effort of lighting it too great, and so he dropped it back on the table. He had a dizzy feeling that many years had passed since he entered that room. Not until Rognaas had found another chair and had been sitting quite still a while, did he ask:

"Have you more to tell?"

Rognaas put his hand over his forehead as if to collect his thoughts.

"Yes," he said. "But I think you had better ask questions after all. My mind is in a whirl."

"How did you escape being caught?"

"By sticking to the plans we had made. The paper said that we had been seen a couple of miles outside the city. Then it was said that this could not be correct, because the cycle had been found just beyond the city limits. Both statements were correct. We separated and came back another way. He went ahead on his own bicycle, which he had hid under a bridge near the place where we stopped, going out. Then I followed him on the motor-cycle, but with light on and a false license number. Near the city border I punctured one of the tires with a piece of bottle glass and walked the rest of the way . . . but along a new route again, through the park. There I picked up a walk that is used a good deal, and it was out of the question that I should be suspected. On the contrary, it was to my advantage to be seen there. During that time he arranged his accident on the bicycle in order to cover up the wound he had received from Lydersen. And there was nothing suspicious about that either. He was passing through the city . . . going in the opposite direction. We had broken open and thrown away the box near the motor-cycle, at the other end of the city."

"Were you not afraid that Lydersen might have recognized you in spite of the mask?"

Rognaas made a negative movement with his head.

"No," he replied, "I knew that I would never enter his thoughts. I had on a leather jacket and overalls, as you may recall. That caused my shape to look different, and, of course, he had never seen me in that kind of outfit. And besides . . . I don't think he saw me at all, and at any rate he didn't hear my voice. But you did. And that's why *you* were the only one I feared."

"Me?"

"Yes, I thought you might remember my voice, and that I might have to wait on you at the bank."

Berger shook his head.

"You could have saved yourself that worry," he said. "I was too badly upset. I couldn't recall the sound of your voice."

Rognaas rose and looked away.

"Yes, I know it," he said.

"You know it?"

"Yes . . . I tried it out."

And he turned toward the astonished, uncomprehending face of Berger.

"Do you recall a rainy night about a fortnight after the hold-up? A man came up to you and asked what time it was."

Berger sighed, heavily and as if he had found it difficult to breathe.

"Was that you?"

"Yes, it was I. And I had arranged it on purpose."

"And if I had recognized you?"

Rognaas shrugged his shoulders.

"I don't know. I know only that I had to know. Otherwise I could not find peace."

Then Berger also rose and laughed a short, forced laughter.

"Well!" he said. "Then it was you to whom I felt so grateful!"

Rognaas appeared startled and bewildered.

"Grateful?"

"Exactly that . . . grateful. You were the only one who had talked to me as if nothing had happened. And I was so far down that even that did me good."

"Does that make you more bitter?"

"No, it is only strange . . . just as it is strange that the first friend I found after Kvisthus . . . should be you!"

And then a sense of bitter resentment did take hold of him.

"Why do you tell me all this? And why have you started this acquaintance? Is it to ease your own conscience while at the same time you tie me hand and foot?"

Rognaas gave a start, stood up very straight, and looked at him without moving. His tortured face was flushed, with a hard look on it.

"Do you know what I feel like just now?" he asked. "I feel like giving back that blow you gave me a while ago. But don't get scared. I should regret it afterward . . . I also."

Then Berger also turned red. A dumb, brooding sense of pain seized him.

"I realize that I misunderstood," he said. "But *why* did you tell me?"

The hardness faded slowly out of Rognaas' features.

"To give you a chance," he said. "A chance to obtain vindication. Before it was only I who had that chance. Now it is you or I who have it. And you are the one to decide between us. That's what I had in mind. You can go to the police tomorrow, if you care. All I ask is that you keep my dead friend outside."

"I don't even know who he was."

"No, but you know enough to enable the police to find out. For that reason I beg you keep silent about everything relating to him."

Berger looked for a long time at Rognaas in a silence that made them feel each other's presence more forcibly than ever. Then his eyes fell. He felt tired and broken.

"No," he said, his voice full of painful resignation.

"No . . . I shall not accuse anybody. If nothing but my humble existence is concerned . . . then no sacrifices will be needed."

"Do you wish me to do it myself?"

Berger shook his head slowly and deprecatingly.

"No," he said. "No . . . I want everything to be as it was."

"Everything?"

Berger looked up for a moment, intense seriousness on his face.

"No, not everything," he replied.

With that he turned and walked away slowly, reluctantly.

Then Rognaas remarked from behind his back:

"I didn't expect it either. I have merely had the devilish misfortune to become very fond of you."

Berger stopped without turning around.

"The same is true of me."

Silence reigned again for a moment. Then Rognaas said:

"Under those circumstances I should like to tell you something more."

"Is there really anything more to tell?"

"Yes, about us . . . about my friend and myself. What I have told so far was only what concerned you. But I should like to tell the rest . . . for our own sake."

This made Berger turn at last.

"Yes," he said, "I shall be glad to listen. But first I have to calm down a little."

7

IT was near twelve before Rognaas resumed his story. The street below had grown more quiet. Only once in a while did a car whizz by, giving new emphasis to the ensuing stillness. Berger and Rognaas were again seated in their original positions at the table. All that separated them was a few feet of air and the top of the table, but they avoided as far as possible looking at each other.

"The fact that we had killed some one, or that, at least, we were directly responsible for a man's death, nearly caused us to break down," Rognaas began. "If we could have done everything over again, taking our punishment for what we had embezzled instead, we would have done so with pleasure and a sense of relief. In addition I had every day to face a reminder of what had happened. It nearly drove me crazy to see that bandage of Lydersen's day after day. And finally I had to ask him to take it off."

"You never told me of that before."

"No, but it was what I did. And he took it off, although I think he hated to do so. It looked anyhow as if he rather enjoyed wearing it. Later I heard of the treatment you had received, and later still you were passed over. What happened on that occasion, I have told you already. But I may as well repeat that I felt thankful, wildly thankful, because you had spared me from having to kill somebody. I did not see my friend again until a fortnight after the hold-up. And then I was barely able to recognize him. Nor can I quite understand how he managed at all to bear up under it. It was hard enough for me. Strange as it may sound, I believe that it really helped him that there were two of us to share the guilt. At any rate, it helped me. And yet, after all, my case was a different one. For what sustained me more than anything else was that he, and not I, had done the killing. His share seemed greater than mine, although in reality that was hardly true. But if he could bear it, I must be able to do so."

After a brief pause, he went on:

"I don't think two human beings ever longed more for each other than we did whenever we were separated. It might as well have happened that we began to hate each other. But it did not turn out that way. And it is his death that is responsible for my sitting here now. If he had not died, I should never have broken down . . . as I have. It began when I was left alone with the memory. What also helped was probably the tragic character of his death . . . and that I was doomed to be a witness to it."

He grew silent again. And Berger asked in a low, cautious tone:

"How did he die?"

"He was lost while we were sailing. But you must never try to discover who he was."

Berger shook his head.

"You may be perfectly sure that I won't."

"He fell overboard, and we didn't take it very seriously because we knew what a good swimmer he was. But he was taken with cramp and went down. We were three in the boat, but I was the only one he called on in that one desperate outcry we heard from him. It seems to me that to this day I can still hear it. Sometimes it wakes me up at night. It echoes in my ears. It was a death cry over what we two had in common."

He pressed his face against the palms of his hands so that his eyes were hidden. Berger was deeply moved and merely gazed at him, not having the courage to speak.

It lasted only a moment. Then Rognaas straightened up and gave his waistcoat a hard pull, as if this movement might help him to shake off his emotion. When he began to talk again, his voice at first had an intentional and artificial hardness.

"It is of no use to get sentimental," he said. "It will bring no one back to life, and it will not undo anything that has been done. And, for that matter, what is the use of feeling any regrets? What has been done will remain done through all eternity, and we cannot wipe out a single second from our lives, no matter how much we might wish to do so. It is even hard to make restitution for a mere fraction of our wrong-doing. We two, he and I, were naïve enough at one time to think it possible to reduce our guilt. No sooner did we feel safe from the police than we exchanged solemn vows to pay back all that we had stolen. It was about eight thousand kroner."

Renewed surprise caused Berger to ask:

"And you really managed to do so?"

"Yes, so we did. But not while he was still alive. And it didn't help anyhow."

Berger stirred uneasily.

"I am not sure that I understand what you mean," he said. "Did you pay back the money?"

"Yes. But it took a long time. You must remember that we also had other, more legitimate debts. But we did what we could. You can see for yourself how I live. That's the way both of us lived . . . as cheaply as possible. And we had to hide the money. It would not do to put it in a bank and then withdraw it when we needed it. That would arouse suspicions. For we had to assume that the return of it would create a big sensation in the papers."

Berger regarded him with astonishment.

"I have seen nothing about it," he said.

"No, but soon you will. The money has not arrived yet."

"But it has been sent?"

"Yes, it has been sent."

Berger looked not only upset but frightened.

"I cannot understand how you dared to do it," he said. "Suppose you are discovered?"

But Rognaas rejoined:

"Nothing will ever be discovered."

This aroused Berger's curiosity.

"How can you be so sure of that?" he asked. "And how did you go about it in order to feel so sure?"

Rognaas considered for a while before he answered. He seemed to wonder about the wisdom of doing so. Then he brushed his hesitations aside.

"It was easy," he said. "I placed the money in a registered letter mailed at the Oslo post-office."

"Addressed to the post-office department?"

"No . . . neither to the department nor to the police. It was addressed to a fictitious name, general delivery, Gjøvik. How long it will have to lie there, I don't know. But I know that finally it will be sent to the dead-letter bureau. There it will be found who is the proper addressee. The money is accompanied by a note explaining when and where it was stolen."

Berger's face expressed deep concern.

"But think only if it should lead to discovery?"

Rognaas deprecated the suggestion once more.

"It is quite out of the question. The registration of a letter for general delivery at Gjøvik cannot possibly attract any attention. No one will remember it a month later. And it will never occur to a single soul to connect me with that letter."

"But the handwriting?"

"First of all they would have to examine every handwriting in the country. Secondly, I did not address the letter in my own hand, of course. I printed everything in Roman letters."

"And how about finger-prints?"

"Well, first of all, my own are not known to the police. And no others will be found. I wore gloves when I bought the paper and the envelope, and also when I wrote the note and the address. I have not even touched the money with my bare hands. And the ink came from the post-office lobby."

He looked up with an attempt at appearing unconcerned, but suddenly he turned red.

"Really, you know, I should have been a rascal, and nothing else."

Berger waved aside the suggestion. And after a brief pause he said:

"I could never have believed that it would be so easy."

"It was not easy at all. We considered all sorts of ways before we found the right one. When your imagination is goaded to the utmost by your instinct for self-preservation, it will hit on the most effective way in the end."

Another pause followed. Berger rose with a desire for moving about. But nevertheless he remained standing on the same spot.

"And now?" he asked.

"Yes . . . and now? That's up to *you* to decide, as I told you a while ago."

Berger shook his head uncomfortably.

"I have given you my answer already."

"But I should prefer that you slept on it. I shouldn't like to take an answer that you might regret later on."

"I shall never regret it."

"Nevertheless I would rather have your answer at some other time. During the next week, I shall wait for you here every night from nine to ten."

"And if I withhold my answer?"

"Then we shall never meet again."

With a heavy mind, Berger nodded agreement.

"I suppose not," he said.

Both had grown visibly nervous. And Rognaas said without looking at Berger:

"In that case I shall leave the country anyhow."

"You will leave the country?"

"I have applied for a position with a Norwegian business house abroad, and I can have it if I want it."

Berger seemed to breathe more easily.

"Take it," he said. "You can do it safely. I shall never change my mind."

"Are you absolutely sure?"

"Yes . . . oh, yes, there can be no doubt about that."

"And you don't think that I ought to give myself up?"

"What good would that do?"

Pale and tormented, Rognaas looked down with an embarrassed expression.

"As an atonement," he said. "To take my punishment."

It sounded as if he had thought of this a long time.

Berger gave him an astonished and pensive glance. Then he shook his head.

"It wouldn't help," he said. "I don't believe in any external atonement."

"And the one within?"

"Yes . . . but I think that one is already achieved."

His own words troubled him, and a moment later he said:

"I have sat here and listened to a confession, but I have no sense at all of being in the company of a criminal. It may sound silly to say so, but time and again I have had the feeling that what you told had nothing to do with us two . . . that it was something that had happened to other people."

Rognaas regarded him attentively. Then his eyes dropped.

"Perhaps you are right," he said.

He remained seated, his hands resting in his lap. Berger stood looking at him for a moment. Then he turned unwillingly and put on his overcoat. There was a brooding and wounded expression on his face, and he had to wait as if to let a pang of pain pass. Then, with his hat in hand, he went over to Rognaas, who raised his eyes when he stopped. His glance was solemn and seemed directed at something far off.

"I am bidding you good-bye now," Berger said. "But it's more like a funeral."

He shook his head with a sense of helplessness. Rognaas rose in silence and held out his hand. Neither one of them could find another word. They shook hands firmly, and let it go at that.

Not until he was about to close the door behind himself did Berger speak again:

"Don't wait for me, as you said you would. It is settled that I shall not come back."

8

THUS, for a second time, something sensational happened to Berger. It did not occur *quite* so suddenly as the first time, and the accompanying external circumstances were not quite so impressive. Nevertheless he felt disturbed and bewildered. His memories and his imagination were stirred to such an extent that he did not even try to master the resulting emotions. He wandered about the streets until late in the night, full of what he had heard. What had impressed him most and now weighed most heavily on him was not the long story told by Rognaas. After all, that was nothing but a rather upsetting explanation of something that had happened eight years before. What hit him with the same horror as when the thing happened and furnished the concentrated explanation in itself were the words spoken by Rognaas: *For I know who killed Kvisthus.* The impression made on him when he first heard those words, and when the truth dawned on him, slowly and terrifyingly—that was what overshadowed everything else.

"I struck him," he thought, "and I could do nothing else. It was the only response I could make.

It was the only thing that could bring me any relief at all. And I think I was right in doing so . . . even if it was too late . . . even if I regretted it afterward."

He crossed a street without knowing why he did so.

"Lord, Lord, what is it that has happened to me tonight?" he moaned inwardly. "I know that a wish of mine has been fulfilled, but if I had known that the fulfillment of it would take such a form, I should never have had the wish.—*He,* too . . . *he!*"

He shook himself and turned his head this way and that . . . as if to get away from it, to rid himself of the whole thing. But it could not be done. It *had* happened. It *was* he himself who was walking there, and he came from a meeting with Rognaas.

IT WAS after two when he got home. Helen was awake when he entered the bedroom. She sat up in the bed, still drunk with sleep, and looked apprehensively at him.

"What are you thinking of?" she asked. "Don't you know that you have to be up at six?"

He merely gave her a reassuring nod and began to undress without looking at her.

"Has anything happened?"

"No."

"You look as if something had upset you."

"Do I? Well, it's nothing at all."

It annoyed him that she continued to watch him. And he felt relieved when he could turn out the light. He turned his back to her and huddled down beneath the covers in order to be alone with what he had just experienced.

Then she asked ... and now she was more fully awake:

"Have you been with Rognaas all this time?"

"Most of the time. I took a walk afterward."

"Had you no idea of how foolish that was, so late at night, when you have to get up early?"

"No," he replied impatiently. "It can't harm any one but myself, can it? And if it makes you feel better, I can tell you that it's all over."

"All over, you say?"

"Yes. He has taken a position abroad."

Then she asked with a touch of jealousy in her voice:

"Is that why you are so down in the mouth?"

"Good-night," he replied, pulling the covers over his head.

But he could not sleep. As soon as he closed his eyes, the events of that evening began to whirl through his brain. In disorderly fashion, without any sequence, the different moments with their attendant impressions popped into his mind. He tried to squirm away from it. He tried to huddle up until it couldn't reach him. But nothing helped. There it was again. And time after time, when despair gripped him too harshly, he was on the verge of breaking into dry and choking sobs.

Then he felt a gentle touch on his shoulder, and a troubled voice asked:

"Erik . . . are you sick?"

"No," he answered brokenly. "No."

"Yes, I believe you are. I think I had better turn on the light."

He made no reply to this as he heard her get up and put on her dressing-gown. Then the room was full of light again. It did help a little after all, and he sat up in bed.

Helen sat down on the edge of the bed, and she had an air of anxiety that did him good.

"Do you care a little for me?" he asked, and his teeth rattled as he spoke.

"Yes, indeed. Yes, of course I do. But what is the matter?"

He merely sighed deeply.

"Shall I wake up the boy and send him for the doctor?"

He shook his head.

"There is no doctor that can help me."

"But what *is* it then?"

"Oh, something has happened."

He looked at her in dumb helplessness, but when he noticed the disturbed expression on her pale face, he took hold of her hand firmly.

"It is nothing serious," he said. "I simply had not expected it."

She stroked his forehead nervously and found it wet with perspiration.

"You had better tell me," she pleaded, and her voice was made unsteady by apprehension and fear.

"Yes," he said, "if you will promise me never to say a word about it to any human being."

He gave her a look that increased her fear still more.

"I will," she said.

Then he took her by the shoulders and buried his face between her soft breasts. And in that way, close to her and yet hidden, he groaned out his confession:

"It was Rognaas who took the money."

Puzzled by his words, she pressed him closer to herself.

"The money?" she repeated.

"Yes . . . *my* money . . . that time Kvisthus was killed."

Then she raised his face so that she could see it.

"Rognaas?"

He gazed back at her as if he had reached the end of his wits and his endurance.

"Yes, that is the truth," he said despairingly. "He told me so tonight. And I'll tell you all about it. But first I must try to calm down a little."

PAINFULLY and with deep emotion he told her everything. When he was through and felt a little more quiet, she asked:

"Did it hurt you so much that it was he?"

"It did," he said. "Do you find that unreasonable? We two had become friends . . . even though we did not know each other very well . . . or on that very account perhaps."

"But you ought to feel relieved."

"So I used to think that I should feel. But it turned out differently." He shook his head. "No, that was not the way I expected it to come about, not the way I wished it to happen."

"And you have made up your mind not to report it?"

"Yes."

For a while he studied her searchingly.

"Has it not occurred to you that it would mean your exoneration?"

"Yes."

"And yet you don't want to do it?"

"No, I don't."

He could see that she disapproved, and he said:

"There were only two places where I craved justification . . . with you and with Lydersen. If I have not achieved it with you tonight, then I can never hope for it."

When he had said that, he looked away, but it was plain that he expected an answer.

"Yes," she said, "I know now that I was mistaken. And I knew it at the time it happened also. But you know how it is when we are tormented by others."

They looked uncertainly at each other.

"Thank you," he said.

For a while they sat close together, shivering a little with the cold.

Then she asked:

"Are you angry at me?"

"No," he answered, "I have never been angry. I

merely wondered that you . . . had to have proofs."

She grew red in the face.

"Won't you forgive me that?"

"Yes," he said.

But he felt a slight pang nevertheless.

V

TWO LIVING AND ONE DEAD

1

THESE were the very days when Postmaster Lydersen assumed his new duties. He received a gold watch from his former colleagues as a sign of their appreciation . . . or "out of thankfulness for his departure," as the youngest clerk in the office put it. This was an indolent and unreliable youngster, and his witticism implied considerable exaggeration, even though it made a big hit in the office.

Lydersen, on the whole, was not a man to be taken too lightly. The passing years had given him a staid and dignified manner, which was merely emphasized by his natural, somewhat boorish unapproachableness. Out of respect for his own years and his seniority in the service, he had developed a small, reddish-brown moustache, which suited him so well that he was quite unthinkable without it. As he continued to be a man shrewd enough to keep silent when there was something he didn't know or didn't understand, he had gradually worked up a certain vague feeling of respect for himself.

Out of sheer inertia he had stayed at the same boarding-house, which in the meantime had changed owners twice. The boarders had changed, too. Of the old guard from Lydersen's heroic days the only ones remaining were himself, Frøken Larsen, the lady who owned the handicrafts shop, and Engelhardt, the engineer. That is to say, the last one had been missing for several years "on account of marriage," as he himself put it, but he had disentangled that connection and returned with his original ego quite unchanged. Unfortunately the junior clerk at the office, Tornfelt, chose to live at the same place, much to Lydersen's chagrin. And there, where he felt happily removed from discipline and seniority, it happened that this youngster allowed himself a degree of comradeship that smacked of impertinence and tactlessness. But fortunately there were chances of getting even with him during office hours. And such chances Lydersen used as effectively as possible and with a robust conscience.

During all those years Lydersen had only once been near getting married. Frøken Larsen had several times tried to direct his attentions toward some of the younger female boarders. But only once had it looked as if the kettle would boil. She had already begun to smile her discreet blessings upon the two young people when Engelhardt appeared on the scene of war. And the unforgivable thing was that he did not act like the proverbial tenor, but like a veritable seducer. In other words, he was led away to be married as a lamb is led to slaughter. When, three years later, without display of any visible damage, he resumed his place at the dinner table, he nodded good-humoredly to Lydersen and explained everything in these words—spoken in the presence of Frøken Larsen at that:

"*You* should have had her . . . you, who are a hero!"

Lydersen turned red and kept silent. But the questions which that word "hero" elicited from several of the uninitiated served nevertheless to bring him a certain recompense. Since Berger's departure from the city it had been difficult to produce any references to the great event, either at the office or at the boarding-house. And although in a manner he had felt it a relief when Berger left, he had missed him all the same. The triumphal chariot had suddenly come to a stop.

Such was the situation the day when Lydersen ceased to be a mere chief of division. The fact alone that it was a day of farewell sufficed to extract him from his every-day obscurity. And on top of this it happened that a new and still greater sensation appeared to resurrect the glory of his period of greatness.

The evening paper brought the sensational news that the money stolen in the hold-up of the post-office had been repaid. Unfortunately the robbers still remained unknown, not having left the least clue behind this time either. Their cunning mode of procedure was described in detail. The letter could be traced by the department from the post-office at Gjøvik back to Oslo. But there the trail was lost. And the note accompanying the money contained nothing but a laconic statement that here it was. No confessions. No expressions of guilty conscience. Nothing but the action itself, quite stark. Nothing but a repayment. The whole thing was highly mysterious.

During the last hours at the office this event was the sole topic of conversation, pursued with great gusto. Lydersen had a chance to explain and relate. He also had a chance to put his candle on top of the bushel once more. And to put Berger's under it.

At seven o'clock he could march off triumphantly. Then the gold watch had also been presented, and he had expressed his appreciation . . . if not with any particular emotion, it was at least with a somewhat shame-faced dignity.

THE event was also discussed after supper in the boarding-house. There were seven or eight persons in the sitting-room, and Frøken Larsen was again granted the privilege of telling about the hold-up and the great impression it had made on everybody. On account of Lydersen's departure, the hostess treated them to a glass of port, and the atmosphere was a little livelier than usual. Perhaps this was the reason why the new sensation proved so startling. In fact, it may have been the reason why it developed. It was staged by Tornfelt, the junior clerk. And he arranged it most effectively as a finale, on top of the impressive pause that followed Frøken Larsen's lecture.

Suddenly he smiled, raised his glass, and bowed to Lydersen.

"May an insignificant colleague be allowed to congratulate the postmaster . . . with all proper respect, of course?"

Lydersen reached for his glass, a little embarrassed, a little displeased because the conversation was already to be given a new direction.

"Thank you," he said, "but it seems to me that you have already done so several times."

Tornfelt smiled again.

"No," he said, "I was not thinking of the appointment. I was thinking of the money that has been returned."

Then Lydersen put away his glass without having touched it.

"What have I to do with that?"

He looked disturbed and angry, and Frøken Larsen hastened to his assistance.

"Yes," she said, "what has he to do with that?"

Tornfelt made another bow with exaggerated civility and blushed at his own cheek. At the same time, however, he smiled . . . probably without malicious intent.

"I beg your pardon," he said, "but I understood that the postmaster also had been robbed of the money in *his* charge."

"Yes . . . and what of it?"

"Please don't misunderstand me. Far be it from humble me to try to belittle the grandiose action of the postmaster. But as he was unfortunate enough to lose the money in his box, the box was useless in my opinion. And so I thought he would be happy to have the money returned."

He made haste to drink, in order to hide the shyness which resulted from having drawn everybody's attention to himself. Then an angel passed through the room, as the saying goes, and very slowly at that.

It was chased off by Engelhardt's queer grimace, which was meant for a smile, and by his ecstatic voice as he raised his glass to Tornfelt and said:

"It is as we Conservatives have always maintained . . . out of the mouths of babes the truth shall be revealed."

Lydersen turned red all over and stared in a rage at the engineer while leaving Tornfelt out of account entirely.

"The truth?" he asked. "The truth, I suppose, is that I was knocked senseless?"

"Yes . . . and that you lost the money."

"Yes . . . and what of it?"

Engelhardt's smile grew broader.

"Exactly," he said. "What of it?"

Lydersen looked around in bewilderment to get some support against this unworthy conspiracy. He turned first of all to Frøken Larsen, teacher of history. And he did not do so in vain. She straightened up and surveyed the class sternly.

"No one," she said, "asks about the *usefulness* of an heroic deed. Even if a great deed should fail, and for that reason prove useless, it is nevertheless a great deed."

Engelhardt bowed politely.

"Of course," he said. "Even our babe, Tornfelt, has not ventured to touch the deed. He has merely permitted himself to call your attention to the fact that it was completely superfluous."

"You seem to forget, Herr Engelhardt, that there is something we call the inspiration of a great example."

Engelhardt folded his hands and placed them piously against the edge of the table.

"That's a different thing," he said. "If Lydersen let himself be knocked senseless in order to inspire other mail clerks to do the same, then I retire and admit my defeat. And I regret deeply that the inspiration of his example did not extend so far as to his nearest colleague . . . Berger I think his name was . . . who did not lose his senses."

General laughter followed. But everything must come to an end, and Frøken Larsen could afford to wait. She smiled sourly:

"It is not for nothing that you are such an eager bridge player, Herr Engelhardt. You are clever at shuffling the cards. The one man who is a coward does not matter. Those who matter are the ones who are *willing* to let themselves be inspired."

Engelhardt turned politely to Lydersen.

"What you did, then, was not done for the sake of the money, but for the sake of the deed itself and the example it would set?"

Lydersen regarded him with ill-tempered suspicion.

"I did it to save whatever could be saved," he retorted curtly. "And for that matter, it is no business of yours, or of any one else, why I did it. So you need not feel troubled on that account."

Engelhardt's face was twisted out of shape by a happy and joyful smile. He snapped his long, thin fingers in ecstasy and nodded to Frøken Larsen in a spirit of cordial understanding.

"Grand slam!" he cried.

Whereupon Frøken Larsen rose and gave Lydersen a peculiarly offended farewell glance. When the last swish of her departure had died away, Engelhardt and Tornfelt arranged a game of bridge. Lydersen was left behind in a troubled mood with the handicrafts lady. They did not exchange a word. Lydersen was preoccupied with Frøken Larsen's glance and, still more, with his own reply to Engelhardt. As far as he could make out, that reply must have been a strategic mistake. But why in hell didn't they leave him in peace . . . both Engelhardt and the old lady?

NEXT DAY he left the city. But he had no idea of the goal toward which he was travelling.

2

THE story of Rognaas was to have results of far greater importance to Berger's final destiny than he could imagine possible at first. During the days between the confession and the return of the money to the post-office department he underwent a radical and remarkable transformation.

The next morning he woke up under the pressure of a gloomy feeling that he had lost the biggest opportunity of his life . . . the opportunity on which he had built all his hopes, on which his entire existence rested. The case would never be cleared up, and the moment would never come when Lydersen would be forced to admit that the humiliations of all those years had been unjustified.

"No," he thought bitterly, "he will go on triumphing over me through all eternity. My own weakness is to blame for it. I know it. But I cannot sell Rognaas for the sake of buying myself free. Now *he* will have a chance at least. And he will be sure to make use of it to the full. Therefore it is better for him and for every one else that he go unpunished. It is better for every one . . . except myself."

Then he observed for the first time that his resentment against Lydersen had grown into something that only could be called hatred. It troubled him, and it frightened him. At the same time he felt concerned on behalf of Rognaas. Several times he nearly made up his mind to look him up again—only to find out how he was getting along. But he managed always to control this impulse, even though he knew that, in spite of everything, he could never uproot that friendly feeling of which he was still conscious.

"It is sheer madness," he had to confess to himself. "When everything is said and done, it is he who must be held responsible for everything. He is responsible for the killing of Kvisthus, and it is because of him that Lydersen has been able to triumph at the expense of my humiliation. And now he has tied me hand and foot."

It happened a couple of times that Helen repeated

her question whether, in spite of all, he would not report the matter to the police.

Then he replied irritably:

"It's not Rognaas I am after. It's Lydersen."

"Lydersen?"

"Yes, Lydersen. Him and no one else. Has Rognaas ever looked down on me? Has Rognaas ever interfered with my rights? I know perfectly well that I cannot recover what I have lost. And I can live contentedly without it. I shall be contented . . . and feel completely exonerated . . . the day I can force Lydersen to see the truth."

She made a discouraged movement with her shoulders.

"That will never happen."

But he replied eagerly and excitedly:

"You don't know that. Anyhow I feel like having a real talk with him once. If I could only figure out the right way of going about it."

Then she remarked, her face strangely rigid:

"Why don't you ask Rognaas?"

He cowered as if she had slapped his face for no apparent reason.

"Rognaas?"

"Yes. It seems to me that he is very clever at . . .

arranging things to suit himself. Perhaps he might also help you."

Berger became blood-red. And he turned away from her, deeply offended both on his own account and that of Rognaas.

And yet ... what followed had its real origin in this casual talk. She had sowed a seed in his mind that began to sprout with a rapidity that bewildered him. He was frightened by the indisputable truth back of what she had said, and he tried to get away from it. But it had already set his imagination on fire. It developed into a sort of nervous fever, and finally into something like a mania.

"If Rognaas could find his way out of so many difficulties," he thought, "I should be able to find my way out of the only one that confronts me. If chance will grant me no help, I should be able to help myself."

He began to study the problem ... hesitantly and gropingly at first, and then with steadily increasing audacity. He visioned many possibilities, but he realized also that none of them was the right one.

If this brooding led to no positive results, it was nevertheless not without consequences ... it served more and more to increase his rage against Lydersen. It became a fixed idea with him that, some time, he must encounter Lydersen and triumph over him, no matter what the cost.

One day Helen asked him:

"What is wrong with you these days? You have grown so pale and nervous."

Irascibly he brushed her question aside.

"Nothing is wrong with me."

Then she studied him earnestly and apprehensively.

"I am frightened on your account. You look as if you might take it into your mind to do something."

He gave her a wry smile.

"Well," he said, "what matter if I did?"

"You must remember that you have a wife and a child."

He replied with a shrug of his shoulders:

"I have remembered that long enough. It is about time that I was permitted to think a little of myself too."

"What do you mean by that?"

"Oh, nothing in particular. I just happened to say that."

He avoided her searching and frightened glance.

"I believe you miss Rognaas," she said suddenly. "Is that it?"

He shook his head.

"No . . . but just the same I am glad he got out of it."

"I can't understand you," she said. "No . . . I can't understand you."

To this remark he had no answer.

A moment later she asked:

"Is he gone?"

"Yes, he left when the paper printed the news about the money."

"How do you know?"

He looked away, embarrassed, and did not reply.

"Did you make any inquiries about him?"

Without looking up he answered:

"I went up to where he lived and found his card gone from the door. There was another card in its place."

"You never told me about that."

Then he looked up with a guilty expression.

"No," he said, "because I was ashamed of it. But I couldn't keep from doing it."

ONE DAY during the spring it suddenly occurred to him what he must do. It came over him in a flash, and the idea terrified him. He was sitting in the mail car at the time and had almost fallen asleep over his accounts. He gave a start and sat up as if some one had called his name. Then he turned hot and flamingly red. His hands began to perspire, and he rubbed them nervously against his linen jacket.

"No," he protested in a state of fright that pervaded his entire being. "No . . . no!"

Completely upset, and regardless of the assistant who was sorting out letters behind him, he rose and stood staring at the rear of the car. His mind whirled in a wild excitement that made him dizzy.

His assistant laid down a bundle of letters and regarded him with sympathy.

"Do you feel sick?"

Then Berger understood that he must pull himself together.

"No, not at all. It was the heat only. But it has passed now, and I think we can do a little more work."

The idea that had flashed into his mind was as surprising as it was startling. It was still a little vague, and at first sight it appeared too risky for execution. But it *could* set him free. Then it took hold of him and began to take definite shape with a rapidity that almost left him breathless. It gripped him firmly, and his imagination could no longer let it go.

Time and again during that day he tried to get

rid of it. But it was of no use. And walking home that night, he found himself working at it deliberately and with fixed determination.

Then he was frightened again.

"Good God," he thought, tormented and wasted by his own excitement, "it must not happen. It might ruin me for the rest of my life."

When he got home, he was more reserved than usual. And then followed a time when he was afraid of himself. While recognizing the risks, he found himself unable to stop working at his plan. It had all the force of a fixed idea. He groaned under it, and tried in helpless despair to push it aside for ever. But the idea was there and demanded execution.

Gradually he became more familiar with it. He began to see that it really could be carried out, and that the day might come when he would take the plunge.

At last Helen made him consult a physician. But nothing was the matter with him. It was all nerves, and the doctor suggested a month's vacation. This suggestion he rejected energetically . . . scared by the thought of being left alone with himself for such a long time.

A FEW weeks later he had an experience that assumed considerable importance and served to strengthen his purpose. He met Esther Kvisthus. That is to say, it was not the Esther Kvisthus he had known once and who was still alive in his consciousness. No, it was quite a different Esther Kvisthus . . . one whom he should never have recognized if she had not spoken to him.

They met at the Eastern Depot. As he was about to pass her, he was startled by her smile of recognition. He stopped halfway only, certain that she had made a mistake.

"How are you, Erik?" she said. "Don't you know me any longer?"

Then he recognized her.

"Is that really you, Esther?"

"No," she replied, "but I am the one who was Esther once. You don't think I resemble her very much. You were about to pass me by."

"Yes," he had to admit. "I guess we have changed a great deal during all these years."

"Not you. You still look like a tall and serious-minded boy."

He tried to smile.

"Do you mean to flatter me?"

"No, it is the truth," she answered. "In the old

days it always seemed to me that you were a boy. And so was Arne."

Berger nodded embarrassed agreement.

"Yes," he said, "so he was."

She sighed and had to look away. It gave him a chance to study her more closely without being noticed. First of all it made him a little sad to see her so simply and cheaply dressed. But what appalled him most was the sight of her face. It was that of a woman who might well be fifty, and he knew that she was not yet forty. Its features were drawn. There was bitterness in it . . . and weariness.

All of a sudden she looked up and caught his disturbed glance.

"Yes," she said, "it is eight years now since he died."

He nodded sympathetically.

"Yes, the time does pass quickly. . . ."

"Quickly? Oh, no . . . to me it seems a hundred years ago."

Her words hurt him, and he suffered a pang of bad conscience at never having looked her up.

"Has it been so hard for you?" he asked, his voice choked.

Her face twitched, and she looked down.

"Hard?" she repeated. "If he could see us here

on earth . . . which I suppose he cannot . . . then he would often weep over what he did. I don't reproach him. No . . . you mustn't believe that I do. For I know that he meant to do his best. But for us it turned out the worst."

In his depression, Berger did not know what to say. But she raised her face and made a movement as if to wipe it all out.

"Don't let us talk about it," she said. "It doesn't help anyhow. But it is true that we miss him. You know yourself how kind he was to us."

Berger looked doubtfully at her two trunks and asked . . . chiefly in order to change the subject:

"Have you been in Oslo? Or have you just arrived here?"

His question seemed to disturb her.

"Neither," she replied. "I am passing through." Then evidently she made up her mind to tell everything: "You may just as well know the truth, Erik. I am on my way to take a place as housekeeper."

He gave a start, surprised and incredulous.

"You?"

She nodded.

"But what about George?"

"It is for his sake I do it. My work in an office barely brought me food. And we were so anxious to give him a good start. You may recall how often Arne talked about it. For this reason I seem to have a double duty."

"Yes, but I cannot understand. . . . What have you done with the boy?"

"He will live with my mother. Now I shall make a little money apart from my board and lodging, and I can save a few kroner. He does his own part by acting as a tourist guide. But he can only give half of his day to it, for he has the school too, poor thing. But he is a splendid boy. He will take his high school examinations this summer."

Again Berger was struck by that pang of bad conscience.

"Esther," he said, "won't you come to see us when you are in Oslo?"

Then she smiled bitterly.

"Who cares for a widow?" she said. "As a rule she is left to go her own way. And so it is good that there are two of us. But we get out very little. And we shall find it hard to be separated."

"I must write down our address for you."

He did so, a little too eagerly, and gave it to her.

"Thanks," she said. "But now I must go, or I shall miss the train. Good-bye for a while, Erik. And remember me at home."

"Thanks. Good luck! And, of course, I must help you with the trunks."

He helped her to find her car, and he stayed with her until the train pulled out. He realized that it pleased her, and it gave him a peculiarly tender satisfaction.

THE PAINFULLY distressing memory of this meeting influenced his attitude toward Lydersen. It gave him occasion to measure the difference in the consequences resulting from that fatal day to the three parties involved in it. And he asked himself:

"Why should he alone gain by it, and we others lose? Why should he advance ... in his own opinion as well as otherwise ... by what put us back? Kvisthus had to die, and his family must be left behind in what is little better than destitution. As for myself, I am reduced for life to a poor overlooked mail clerk. But Lydersen has received both honor and promotion without having earned either. For eight years I have been ass enough to accept everything. It is about time that I did something. He will not be the only one who escapes unscathed."

When he told Helen about his meeting with Fru Kvisthus, his wife listened to him with a blanched, unhappy face and without an attempt at interruption. But when he was through, she burst into tears.

"Poor Esther!" she cried. "Poor Esther!"

Then he looked at her meaningly.

"You might have been in her position if things had gone according to your wish that time."

"No, Erik! I never wished anything of the kind."

But the old sense of resentment burst forth and made him hard.

"Yes, you did," he said. "There were only two things to choose between . . . the fate of Esther . . . or the fate that is yours now."

She looked pleadingly at him.

"I know that I wronged you terribly. But can't you try to forget it?"

He leaned his head in his hand, hiding his eyes. Then he closed them and sat for a long time immovably in the resulting darkness.

"Yes," he replied at last, "I think I can forget it. In fact, I have done so already . . . under ordinary circumstances. But just now it was brought back to my mind so forcibly. After this I shall never mention it again."

And he never did. He bore everything alone, but every passing day made it clearer to him that he could not go on in that way much longer . . . that he must find some sort of escape, of relief, no matter what the cost . . . if he was to go on living at all. Over and over he returned to his plan, studying it from every angle, weighing all its possibilities . . . good and bad alike.

"I must not throw away what still is left for the sake of a rash impulse," he told himself warningly. At the same time, however, he had a frightening premonition that some day his plan would be carried into effect.

"Besides," he tried to reassure himself, "everything may be changed. It is not at all certain that his view of it is the same today. And under all circumstances I must have a talk with him first. Perhaps nothing else will be needed."

This latter possibility increased his temptation. He also figured out that his summer vacation would come at the most convenient time, or about the first of July. On St. John's Eve, Helen and Leif were going to the country, and he himself would follow them a week later. Everything fitted in, and the rest was now up to him.

He couldn't help recalling what he had said to Helen:

"I must soon get a chance to think a little of myself also."

At the same time he was pressed by a chilling fear:

"It is not at all like me. Can this *be* me? Have I suddenly grown foolhardy after having lived a lifetime in cautious obscurity? Perhaps I must say of myself what Esther Kvisthus said: This is not me, but the one I used to be once upon a time."

3

WHEN St. John's Eve arrived, Berger took Helen and the boy to the train. Then he went home... alone, but accompanied by a tremendous temptation. No sooner were the other two gone than the fire that had been smouldering within him for months broke into open flame. It did not surprise him, and it did not take away his breath. On the contrary, it made him more composed. It was as if he had known all the time that his plan would be carried out.

His new state of mind enabled him to work out his scheme in a more realistic and systematic way than before. And as everything began to dovetail in his mind, down to the minutest detail, he became filled with a joyful, anticipatory suspense. It was as if his imagination had rejoiced and wallowed in being used on a large scale for the first time. Sometimes he would stop while walking around the room and rub his hands in a sort of superhuman exaltation that filled him with ineffable bliss. It happened also, however, that a vertiginous fear shot through him, chilling him to the bone. But that lasted only for a brief moment and was nothing but an inevitable reaction from his exultant mood.

He wrote to Helen that he had been delayed a few days. On the first day of his vacation he left in a state of high impatience at having it all over.

He reached his destination the next morning. The first thing he did was to visit the post-office for the purchase of a few stamps. He used the occasion to look around, having ascertained in advance that the private rooms of the postmaster were on the upper floor. Fortunately Lydersen was not to be seen. At the stamp window he found no one but a young man he did not know. Next he discovered that the office of the postmaster was to the right of the main office, with a street entrance of its own through a narrow hallway, and with a window facing the yard in the rear. He ventured into the hallway and found that it ended in a stairway leading to the second floor. Going out, he noticed that the door was equipped with a spring-lock.

All this suited him perfectly. So did the fact that, according to a notice on the door, the office hours during the afternoon were from four to seven.

Reassured in a way, and yet on edge with excited suspense, he started on a long walk beyond the city limits. He spent the whole day in the country, in order not to be seen. During those long hours he yearned nervously for action . . . to be done with the transitory existence, full of uncertainty and danger, into which he had plunged. But his memories of the last eight or nine years gave stamina to his determination. That kind of thing neither could nor would go on for ever.

THAT DAY also came to an end. And when he passed the post-office again, he found it closed.

"I shall wait another half hour," he decided. "He will undoubtedly have supper first. Then he will return to tackle his quarterly report. That will be the time."

Then a thought flashed through him: "Unless he has already done it during office hours."

But he rejected the idea.

"He is too indolent for that. It would be more likely that he let it go for another couple of days . . .

in which case I'll stay here until he can postpone it no longer."

He waited until his watch showed a quarter to eight. Then he gathered himself together with an effort and ascended firmly the steps in front of the street entrance. But the door was locked. He had not counted on this and had to think a little before he rang the bell. He waited in a state of almost unendurable suspense, but no one responded. After having rung again with the same result, he stepped out on the sidewalk and looked up at the windows. To his surprise he saw that the shades were drawn.

As, baffled, he turned around to go, he ran straight into Lydersen. Both of them stood stock still, equally surprised at seeing each other.

Berger was the first to pull himself together... but only by a violent exertion of will power.

"How are you?" he said. "I came to pay you a visit. Don't you live here?"

Lydersen continued to look embarrassed.

"No," he replied, "those rooms are occupied by the retired postmaster for the time being."

"But I rang the bell twice."

"The whole family have gone into the country."

Berger came near smiling, but checked himself in time.

"I thought I might look you up," he said, "seeing that I had a little vacation."

Lydersen's face took on a concerned expression. "This particular evening I have to close up my accounts and write my report," he said. "Are you not staying here over tomorrow?"

"No, but it's all right. I won't interfere with your work. I'll just come inside for a few minutes, and then I'll be going again."

Lydersen nodded curtly, as if confronted with something inevitable. Then he unlocked the door and entered ahead. When they had reached the office, he said:

"We shall not be alone anyhow. My assistant will be here at eight to help count the stamp supply."

Berger hesitated a moment before he remarked in a casual tone:

"If you care, I can help you with that. Then you can let him off. I have nothing else to do anyhow."

Lydersen had no objection to that arrangement. When the assistant arrived a moment later, he was, to his great joy, told to go back home. In the meantime the other two had begun to take everything out of the safe. Berger got hold of a table where he could count the stamps. Lydersen sat at his own desk with the money and the various blanks. His back was turned toward one of the longer walls, and the desk was between him and the rest of the room.

They exchanged a few words now and then while Berger was counting. At nine he was already done with it and asked with some surprise:

"Why in the world did you call on the assistant at all? That was only a few minutes' work."

Lydersen looked a little disturbed as he put down his pipe.

"I should think you need not ask that question," he said. "I don't like to be alone here with the money. One story of that kind was enough for me."

Berger straightened up.

"Do *you* say that?"

"Yes . . . of course."

"You who have had nothing but gain from it? What do you think I should say then?"

"You have no longer any money to be responsible for."

Berger laughed abruptly and harshly.

"No," he said, "you are right there. On that very account I am no longer responsible for any money."

Suddenly he began to walk restlessly back and forth in front of the desk, while Lydersen regarded him disapprovingly. At last he stopped and gave the other one a long look.

"I'll tell you something," he said, "frankly and honestly. That's the very reason why I am here tonight. It is true that I have a vacation. But I decided to use it not merely to look you up, but to get a chance for a real talk with you at last."

Lydersen had turned pale, and the lines around his mouth showed anxiety and irritation.

"A real talk?" he repeated. "I don't understand what you mean."

"No, I know you don't. To you it seems natural that things should be as they are. You feel safe and on top. But it does not seem natural to me. I don't begrudge you anything, but why should everybody begrudge me the least advantage? Have I been guilty of any crime? Or of any disreputable act?"

Lydersen said nothing.

"Oh, I see that you think I have. Well, I knew that before, and it's the main reason for my being here. You are not alone in thinking that, but I can do nothing with the world at large. During all these years, it is you who have stood in my mind as a representative of all the others, partly because you showed most clearly what you thought, and partly because you were a party to what happened and gained by it. For that reason I have never been able to regard you with indifference. I have used you to measure my own humiliation. It was your advance that furnished the measure. If what happened had not happened as it did, I should now be sitting in that chair. It would be *my* pipe lying on the desk, *my* hat hanging on that hook. No, it's useless for you to protest. You know that I am right."

"Well . . . and what of it?"

"What did that happening really have to do with us two . . . professionally I mean?"

Lydersen assumed a somewhat arrogant mien.

"Have I ever said it did?" he asked. "It is you who are getting excited, and who act as if it did have anything to do with us."

Berger let out a sigh of impatience.

"Heavens!" he cried, as if hopeless of making himself understood. "The very reason that I am here is just because it has been and still is assumed that it had something to do with our professional standing. You ought to see that I am not the one who looks on it in that way . . . least of all *now*. But you know perfectly well what part it has played in our relative positions from the day we were called into the postmaster's office to render our reports. You got the praise and I got the rod. And during what followed, you became the hero and I the coward. The consequences were not only economic, but they touched my honor directly. You passed on, and I was passed over. And all this for no other reason than that I happened to be the more sensible one of us two."

Lydersen shoved aside the papers in front of him with a sudden movement. He had grown red in the face.

"You have hashed that up before," he said sharply, "and you need not trot it out again."

But Berger had reached a point where he could no longer be checked.

"Think of Kvisthus," he said. "He did exactly what you did. Do you think that was sensible? Do you believe he would think so himself, if he had a chance to speak? But I suppose he was as much taken by surprise as you were. Perhaps he also resisted out of sheer fright and hysteria."

"He *also?*"

"Yes, that's what I said. Do you seriously believe I could be fooled into thinking that you were moved by any sort of heroic impulses?"

"As far as I am concerned, you can think what the devil you please. All the same, your envy will never succeed in belittling what I did."

"Do you really think I envy Kvisthus?"

"No one has talked about Kvisthus."

"Yes, I have. You and he are in exactly the same class. If you are a hero, then he is another. But I believe he would be glad to exchange, if he had the chance to live the life of a poltroon like myself. What has he got to show for what he did? If you can show me, I shall beg your pardon and leave."

Lydersen regarded him coldly, with his customary sullen dignity.

"I think we might as well let Kvisthus rest in peace where he is," he said.

"As you prefer to evade my question, it means that you can't answer it, I suppose."

"At any rate I can answer you that he died with honor."

Berger nodded.

"Yes," he said, "he did. But, Lydersen, that honor was expensive. You gave him a fine obituary. You were deeply moved when you cheered his memory. But afterward? Is there one among you who has thought of him since then? Is there one among you who has recalled that he had a wife and a child who were dependent on him, and who were left behind in what practically amounted to penury?"

A brief silence ensued. Berger waited tensely, but Lydersen took his time while he met the other one's glance with supercilious contempt. At last he said:

"I suppose no one is brave for the sake of the money alone."

Berger laughed exultantly and harshly.

"Oh, yes!" he cried. "It was just for the sake of the money you showed such bravery. It was for the sake of four hundred kroner that you risked your life. Or *was* it not?"

"Who has talked about that money? You understand very well what I meant."

"Yes, I may as well agree with you. No one is brave for the sake of the money alone. No, indeed . . . but how about those who, according to this calculation, should profit most by the risk taken? How about those who were the real cause of the bravery, the sacrifice, and the loss of a life? Should they not . . . as the least and meanest acknowledgment . . . take care that the survivors were not left to suffer distress? The wife and son of Kvisthus lost *him*. Wasn't that sufficient loss on their part? Is it reasonable that they should also be made to pay in cash for having lost him?"

Lydersen shook his head in displeasure.

"You exaggerate, as you always do. They have their pension, and you know that very well."

"Yes . . . and what is it? One-third of his salary. A couple of months ago I had a talk with Fru Kvisthus. She had placed the boy . . . who also has to work as a tourist guide . . . with her old mother. She herself has been forced to accept a position as housekeeper in order to get a living. That is how they treat the *dead* hero, while the *living* one is made a postmaster. Is this reward granted him because he escaped with life and limbs intact? Let us suppose that you had been sufficiently injured to be rendered incapable of further work. What would your reward have been then? A pension on which you could not have lived. The case is the same as when a war comes to an end . . . the crippled heroes themselves have to pay the cost of the war. With stirred hearts and beating pulses we cheer them. We arrange touching ceremonies in memory of those that have died. But we assume no responsibilities in regard to those that live on."

Lydersen leaned back against the wall and looked at Berger.

"You have grown quite eloquent," he said.

"Yes, you can sneer as much as you please. It doesn't hurt me. It is so utterly unimportant in comparison with the essential facts. And if I show any eloquence, it is probably because I have had plenty of time to prepare myself. I am not improvising now. I have thought of these things for close to nine years now. But it is quite possible that I have let myself become a little too excited. I shall try to be more calm."

He seated himself, wholly exhausted, leaned his head helplessly in one hand, and stared at the floor. Lydersen watched him for a moment. Then he rose with quiet dignity and turned on the light. Later he went over to the window and pulled down the shade. All this was carried out with a certain deliberate indolence, as if he was anxious to prove that he had a good conscience and was afraid of nobody.

When he had seated himself again, Berger looked up. There was a suggestion of pain and sadness on his face.

"Can you remember Kvisthus?" he asked.

The other one nodded with evident embarrassment.

"No one was closer to him than I . . . apart from his own family. And I have thought of him so often. He was so very much alive, through and through. What he did that time was perhaps no more than what you did, but it was no less either. And now he has been rotting in his grave for nine years, while you have been going around here alive and full of conceit on account of the same event that killed him. Have you never thought of that?"

Lydersen turned a shade paler, but his voice reflected an effort at contemptuous dismissal of what had just been said.

"No," he replied, "I have never nourished that kind of maggots in my head."

"Maggots?"

"Yes, that's what you are full of . . . maggots, and a lot of envy."

Berger shook his head gently.

"I have never envied Kvisthus," he said. "And do you know what conclusion I have reached? I believe that there never was a man who risked his life and lost it . . . even to save some one else . . . who would not have refrained if he had known the outcome."

"Yes . . . if he had known it."

Berger gazed firmly at the other one.

"*I* knew it."

Lydersen shrugged his shoulders.

"If it gives you any pleasure to excuse yourself in that way . . . why, I have no objection."

Berger rose and began to walk back and forth in front of the desk. His former restlessness had returned. But suddenly he stopped still.

"Excuse myself?" he repeated. "What have I done that calls for any excuses?"

"Quite right . . . you did nothing."

Placing his hands on the desk, Berger leaned over toward Lydersen.

"Yes, I did," he said. "I protected my life."

"Yes . . . your own!"

"Did I have any other life to protect?"

Lydersen pushed his hand through his hair in nervous bewilderment. He had preserved his closely growing, reddish-brown head of hair, and after that movement it stood straight up like a crop of grass. His eyes glinted with venomous irritation.

"You talk and talk," he said. "You said that you might have been sitting where I am sitting now. But you didn't even dare to put in an application!"

"Yes, that's right, I didn't dare. *Dare* is the proper word. The reason was that I knew the outcome in advance, and I could not permit you to triumph over me again."

"Triumph? What are you talking about?"

"What's the use of pretending? You are the same as ever. You have not changed a bit. You continue to despise me because I would not let myself be killed that time. You still maintain that I disgraced myself. And I came here to discover if that still was your attitude. I hoped that such was not the case . . . for two reasons. One of these was that I am tired of feeling humiliated. I want you to know that I can stand it no longer . . . and that I don't care what else may happen."

Lydersen's glance became unsteady in the face of the other one's suppressed but nevertheless palpable excitement.

"You talk as if it were my fault entirely," he said. "Do you really believe that no one else holds the same opinion?"

"Who has suggested anything of the kind? But to me you represent all the others. To me you stand for all there has been of insolence and of neglect. It is you who have humiliated me, and it is you who have forgotten what was owed to Fru Kvisthus. What am I? A poor mail clerk who will never be anything else. Do you expect me to plead my case against all the world? No, it is from you that I shall seek vindication!"

The face of Lydersen flushed a deep red.

"Do you know what I think?" he asked irascibly. "I think that you have gone crazy!"

Berger nodded energetically.

"Yes, that's exactly what has happened. I *am* crazy."

He turned around abruptly, went over to the window, pulled the shade aside and looked out. Lydersen sat watching him in a daze. And when Berger remained standing at the window, he asked:

"Are you looking for somebody?"

Berger turned and crossed the room without answering. At the door he stopped and turned again toward Lydersen.

"I merely took a look at the yard outside," he said. "It is a large one, and there is a still larger garden between it and the street. Beyond the garden is a tall fence."

Lydersen sat up with evident symptoms of nervousness.

"What do you mean by that?" he demanded, and his voice was fraught with apprehension.

"I merely wished to bring this to your attention. And above us . . . the second floor . . . is standing empty."

Lydersen rose quickly.

"What in hell do you mean?"

Berger gave him a cold and composed glance, but his voice sounded forced when he spoke:

"You'll know very soon. But first of all I must tell you one thing . . . namely, that you had better stay where you are without trying to raise an outcry. For if you do that . . . then you will be *dead*."

Lydersen gave the desk one push to get by, but a

single glance at the other one was enough to make him quit. With eyes that bulged, and dripping perspiration, he stood staring at Berger, who was watching him, keenly and angrily, with a revolver in his hand.

Then Berger added:

"You need not be afraid. I have not come here to kill you . . . that is, unless you prefer to be killed."

Lydersen leaned heavily against the desk, supporting himself with both hands.

"What do you mean?" he asked hoarsely.

"That you will learn later on. Sit down now!"

Lydersen hesitated a moment. Then he slid slowly back into the chair. His eyes did not leave the other man. Both of them were equally white in the face.

"Have you really gone crazy?"

"I told you so a while ago. But don't let it scare you. Nothing will happen as long as you remain quiet. I have not come here to murder you."

"What have you come for?"

With raised gun, ready to shoot, Berger came a step closer. Then he pointed with his left hand to the cash box on the desk.

"I came for that," he said. "So far you have been Lydersen. Tonight it is *your* turn to be Berger . . . or Kvisthus. You can choose for yourself."

Lydersen stared at him, swallowing hard.

"Is that a joke?" he asked.

There was a steady fire in Berger's voice, something assured and inflexible.

"No," he said. "Life is the stake for both of us. I have not come this far merely to frighten you. I have come to get the money or to kill you. The choice is up to you. The money will be mine in any case."

Lydersen's face changed. His features seemed strangely rigid.

"You had better stop now," he said. "All this is simply stupid."

A hard, menacing gleam appeared in Berger's eyes.

"Why do you think it stupid?"

"You will be arrested inside of twenty-four hours."

Berger smiled scornfully.

"Do you suppose I have failed to provide against that? Do you think I have merely planned to put the box under my arm and walk out?"

Lydersen's face suddenly turned gray.

"What have you planned?" he asked, his voice trembling.

Slowly, and with enjoyment, Berger took his measure.

"You are mistaken," he said. "My plan is not to

kill you and take the money as well. It is one thing or the other . . . unless you force me to do both. And it is you who must choose. When I am gone . . . if you let me have the money . . . you must go straight home and keep absolutely quiet. You will not report me until two days have passed."

"Who is going to prevent me?"

"I."

Lydersen gave him a hateful glance.

"You have the power now," he said. "Do you think you'll also have it when you are gone?"

"I do. I have my passport and other documents ready, and I need those two days. Therefore . . . if tomorrow or the day after I should learn that you have reported me, then I . . . no matter where I happen to be . . . will see to it that you are dead before they get me. And if my plan should miscarry, I shall be free again after a while. That's one thing you must bear in mind."

Lydersen still tried to fix his eyes on Berger, but they fluttered with fright and drooped.

"Do you remember that you have a wife and child?"

"That's none of your concern! Nothing of mine concerns you . . . except my decision to make you feel what it is to be a coward. It will be your turn today . . . even if I have to pay with my freedom for it. I have no other choice. I *must*. And I have use for the money. There shall be an end to the miserable and humiliating existence I have led all these years. I also wish to feel like a human being for once."

Lydersen rose abruptly.

"You dare not shoot," he said.

But the wild look on Berger's face, and the sudden raising of the revolver so that it pointed straight at his own forehead, made Lydersen halt.

"Dare not, you say? I am capable of shooting you regardless of the money. Take another step, and you'll find it out. But now this must come to an end. Sit down!"

Lydersen sat down unsteadily, and Berger went on:

"I'll give you five minutes to think it over. When the clock on that wall shows seven minutes past ten you will have made up your mind."

During five long minutes those two watched each other closely. Both were in a state of inner tumult. One was surcharged with excited suspense, the other one with impotent wrath.

Suddenly Berger broke the silence:

"You have one minute left!"

His words were accompanied by a clicking sound

from the gun. It made Lydersen turn red in the face. His eyes became glassy, and his body sagged in the chair. Then he tried to pull himself together.

"Take it," he said in a hard voice.

But Berger remained immovable.

"Push the box over to this side of the desk, as far as you can reach. Then put your hands in your pockets."

Lydersen gave a start. He hesitated.

Then Berger cried in a rage:

"Hurry up! I'll be damned if I'll wait any longer!"

But it was the nerve-racking vision of the gun muzzle that settled the matter. Without a word Lydersen pushed the cash box across the desk and buried his hands in his pockets. His look was that of a mortally wounded beast when Berger approached slowly, with gun still raised. His body shrank as beneath a blow when the box was lifted from the desk and carried over to the stamp table.

And all that time Berger did not take his eyes off him.

"I have no use for the box," he said. "It's the money I want."

His nervousness showed plainly while he emptied the box.

"How much is it supposed to be?"

Lydersen did not reply.

Then Berger counted the money with feverish haste.

"It's about ten thousand kroner . . . if you are interested in knowing."

Still Lydersen refused to speak. He sat stiffly, as if nailed to the chair, and merely stared at what was going on.

Then a sudden change came over Berger. He lowered the gun. All signs of excitement disappeared. He stood looking at the other one with a thoughtful, almost childlike expression on his face.

"Lydersen," he said.

His tone was that of an ordinary call . . . as if everything that went before had been wiped out.

Lydersen's sullen and heavy face twisted painfully, but still he did not answer.

Then Berger said:

"Do you really think that I have any use for that money of yours? What I did have use for was to make you feel, for once, what it has meant to me. Now you have been in my place . . . in the place where I was that time. And perhaps you are no longer a hero. And perhaps I am no longer a cowardly poltroon."

There was no sign of a sneer in his voice. It was indulgent and resigned.

Lydersen stared at him, puzzled and agitated. Then a sense of shame made his face turn scarlet. He wanted to speak, but could not utter a word.

Then Berger picked up the cash box and the money and carried it all back to the desk.

"Here you are," he said. "You are welcome to it, and to the revolver also."

He put down the gun beside the box. But he had barely let it go, when Lydersen made a quick grab at it. And suddenly a changed Lydersen was standing there, his body very straight, his face distorted by hate.

"I'll be damned if you don't deserve to be shot down on the spot!"

Berger smiled, but said nothing.

"There is no reason for you to smile. Tomorrow you will be arrested, you damned rascal!"

But Berger remained as calm as ever and merely looked at him.

"Not when you have slept on it," he said. "Now I am the only one who knows about it. And if I don't care to expose you, I suppose you won't."

"You know nothing about it."

Berger nodded.

"Yes, I do. You will realize how ridiculous it would make you."

"I am no more ridiculous than you were, and if you could stand it, I can. You are feeling a little too secure now. But I'll sacrifice everything to settle you for ever, plain bandit that you are!"

Once more Berger smiled a peculiarly weary smile.

"You will appear far more ridiculous than I did," he said. "First of all because you knew me, and knew that I am not such an idiot as I have pretended to be. And secondly because . . . that revolver has never been loaded."

The shock of this stunned Lydersen. His face became blank and helpless. Then he looked incredulously at the gun, which was still in his hand.

Then he looked up threateningly.

"You lie," he said.

And with a quick movement he pointed the revolver toward the ceiling and pulled the trigger.

Nothing was heard but a faint click.

Then he threw it away and sat down heavily.

A moment's pause followed. Then Berger spoke again.

"Now you know how it feels," he said. "And you know also that life is more important than a bunch of bills. All of a sudden we two have been placed on an equal footing... and neither one needs any longer to look down on the other one."

When he stopped, Lydersen looked up with a certain timidity.

"Isn't that what you are doing now?"

But Berger shook his head.

"No," he said. "I did not come here to humiliate you. I came here to get justice for myself... to get justice from you, who have humiliated me more than any one else. I don't care about the others."

He turned slowly, picked up his hat, and made for the door. Having opened it, he turned around again.

"Good-night," he said quietly. "I shall not ask you to forget this. On the contrary, I should like you to remember it. But I should also like you to know that I harbor no grudge against you any longer. It vanished together with your heroic courage."

Lydersen gazed at him, but said nothing. When the door had closed behind Berger, he remained sitting where he was... as if he couldn't understand, couldn't grasp what had happened. His brain went on a strike in the face of what seemed incredible. He had lost an essential part of his old self, and he found it hard to become reconciled to what had appeared in its place.

He had suddenly changed into another man... one who was unknown and unfamiliar to him... one for whom he could have no admiration, but of whom he was a little afraid and a little ashamed.

At last he rose reluctantly and went over to pick up the revolver.

A faint and tiny hope was still alive within him.

Without giving much thought to what he was doing, he raised the weapon once more toward the ceiling and fired.

Still nothing was heard but that same faint click.

Then he put it down beside the box. A moment later he crossed the room and locked the door. But he could no longer bear being alone in that empty house. In a state of mind bordering on panic, he shoved the money and the stamps back into the safe.

Then he went home to his boarding-house, hoping that it might bring back his sense of security.

4

BERGER took a long walk while waiting for the train. He also felt like a new man. But in that feeling there was no sense of triumph. He had won no glorious victory. He had merely achieved a belated vindication. And he yearned to be with his own . . . yearned to tell them all about it . . . not for the sake of any sensation, but merely to be done with it once for all, so that he might begin to live again like an ordinary human being . . . like the man he was before the hold-up.

He did not reach Helen and the boy until the next morning . . . a little worn and tired by the long journey.

Helen looked at him with surprise.

"Anything wrong?"

He shook his head quietly.

"Have you been sick?"

"No."

"You are pale, and you look all in. Were you unable to sleep last night?"

"I hardly slept at all."

It made her visibly nervous.

"What *is* it then?"

"I have been to see Lydersen."

"Lydersen?"

"Yes . . . I'll tell you all about it when we are by ourselves after dinner."

He went out to join Leif, leaving her utterly puzzled. A presentiment of evil began to take hold of her. But it vanished when she happened to take a look at those two. They had made themselves bows and arrows and were using an old hat as a target. They were laughing and enjoying themselves like two small kids.

Then she understood that he had profited by his visit. But she remained as anxious as ever to hear what he had to tell.

When the dinner was over, he told her everything, as he had promised.

He related everything quietly, soberly, without any exaggeration, and she listened for a long while in a state of choking suspense that kept her speechless. Then her mind grew more easy, but even when he had finished, she remained somewhat frightened at what he had done.

"How did you dare?" she burst out. "And what made you think of it?"

"It just came," he said. "And I had to do it."

He looked at her earnestly and whispered:

"I have had such a hard time."

She went over and patted his hair tenderly.

"Yes, you have had a hard time," she said. "And I am glad it is over. But I cannot yet understand where you found the courage to take such a risk."

"Nor can I."

She turned up his face toward her own and regarded him with a smile.

"You must have been crazy."

He tried to nod, but her hands held his face with a firm grip.

"Yes," he said, "I have been crazy these last nine years."

A moment later he added: "I understand that now . . . now that I am sane again."